Everyone – even ̶h̶i̶s̶ ... ̶s̶e̶e̶s̶ ̶C̶l̶a̶u̶d̶i̶n̶e̶
de Trévires as a meek schoolgirl, too innocent to realise
what it means to live in French-occupied Luxembourg in
1789. But at a time when another Revolution is trying to
sweep away the little duchy, Claudine is brave enough, to
give shelter and help to the rebel leader, the Marked Man,
whom the French are determined to capture.

At first it seems vaguely romantic for a young girl to
give help to a revel, but Claudine swiftly learns that the
attractive fugitive is also the wicked Comte de Villerange,
of whom she has heard such dreadful stories. All too soon,
she too is in danger – the danger of falling in love with him.

The Marked Man

Meriol Trevor

MILLS & BOON LIMITED
London · Sydney · Toronto

First published in Great Britain 1974 by
Hodder and Stoughton Limited, 47 Bedford Square,
London WC1B 3DP
This edition published 1979 by
Mills & Boon Limited, 17–19 Foley Street,
London W1A 1DR

ISBN 0 263 72713 0

Filmset in 10pt Plantin

Made and printed in Great Britain by
C. Nicholls & Company Ltd.,
The Philips Park Press, Manchester

CHAPTER ONE

THE two sisters started out together, but they had hardly crossed the parterre when Seraphine was called back by one of the teachers.

"What have I forgotten now?" she exclaimed, making a face. "You go on, Claudine, up to the ruins. I'll catch you up."

And she ran back along the paths between the flower beds – bare because it was November, although such a mild day that the girls were making for their favourite haunt, the ruins of the old castle of Villerange.

Seraphine ran, swinging her hat in her hand, her mop of yellow curls flying free, back to the great château, built foursquare round a courtyard, in which a school for girls, run on enlightened principles, had been founded after the flight of its owners in the Revolutionary Wars. She was sixteen, and her sister two years older, but they were left at school by their father, Monsieur de Trévires, a republican in sympathies, because he was its founder and supporter. Their mother agreed because she did not think the present situation in Luxembourg was quite suitable for bringing her daughters out into society.

Claudine climbed slowly up the steep path to the ruins, thinking about the peasants' rebellion. For this was 1798, and it was three years since the fortified city of Luxembourg had yielded to the French Revolutionary Army, the Austrian garrison had marched away, and the Tree of Liberty been planted in the Place d'Armes. The ancient duchy, once part of the Holy Roman Empire, had been incorporated in the new France and was governed by a Commissaire and a bureaucracy of officials and police, with soldiers stationed there to hold down the people of a country which had no sympathy either with the French or with their revolutionary principles. This year, when conscription had been introduced, the peasants had revolted and there had been fighting in September and October.

It was hopeless, of course, for what could peasants, some armed only with wooden staves, do against seasoned troops? It was terrible to hear of the slaughter and almost worse to hear of the young men rounded up, marched off to Luxembourg and thrown into the dungeons there. A guillotine was set up, just as in Paris; the prisoners were brought before tribunals and many were sent to execution. Claudine had wept at night, thinking of this terror.

And now the soldiers were in the villages, disarming everybody, hunting for rebels, some of whom were still hiding in the woods. The officials called them brigands.

The headmistress, Madame Bilsdorf, called them brigands too. The girls were warned not to go beyond the gardens, for fear the brigands might carry them off. Seraphine had immediately become very keen to take a long walk in the woods. It was a moot point whether the ruins were in the garden or not; they were up on a ridge, and the woods began on the other side of the steep ravine which they overlooked. Seraphine hoped some rebels might come up there; Claudine was sure they would not. But she was thinking of them that November afternoon, as she climbed up among the broken walls and crumbling towers of the medieval castle, once the fortress of the robber counts of Villerange, the proud family of Erlen.

Claudine was taller than Seraphine; she was even a little taller than her father, which embarrassed her when she was walking with him, for she had a great respect for his wisdom. But she was not the tallest girl in the school, though she was the eldest; nor, to her shame, considering whose daughter she was, did she often reach the top of the class.

"Don't dream, Claudine!" Mademoiselle Charpentier would say sharply.

It was true, Claudine did dream; her mind was often far away from classrooms and lessons. She might be thinking about the Revolution – why republican ideals, which she accepted from her father as the best, should have issued in violence against the simplest of the people. But she might just be trying to remember the words of a song. She had a clear sweet voice, but was too shy to sing by herself in public.

Now, when she reached the level ground, she began to sing an old ballad in the Germanic dialect of the country, which she had learned as a child, though brought up, like most people of good family, to speak French. France had once been the home of all that was civilised.

The November sun glinted on the grass, green after rain. Claudine walked to the edge of the plateau and stood in a broken archway, looking across the steep valley to the woods on the other side of the deep narrow river that ran below. In this thin slanting light the golden leaves still on the trees gleamed; even a crimson-leaved cherry she saw, far down the slope.

Claudine pulled off her hat and shook her hair free. A silky golden brown, it waved back in heavy locks to her shoulders. Monsieur de Trévires believed in the beneficial effects of Nature, and both girls were sturdy and graceful. Claudine had a creamy skin, but not pale. Her face was quiet and gentle, not soft, and she had large serious grey eyes under wide dark brows.

The ballad was still running in her head. It had a sad farewell quality which appealed to her youthful sense of romantic melancholy. She sang the refrain again, throwing her voice across the valley, and suddenly became aware there was an echo.

From the golden woods opposite her own voice, sounding not her own, came back to her with the last syllables of the phrase she sang. It was strange – as if there was someone else there, an invisible dryad echoing her.

Claudine began to play with the echo, calling out words and listening to the faint, the hollow reply. Sometimes she sang them and they sang back, a falling note. It was a double echo: she could hear a word of two syllables return.

"*Attendez, fantôme!*" she called.

"*Fantôme!*"

It sounded so eerie, that ghost, that she suddenly recalled all those recently dead, killed because they would not fight for the Revolution, for the French. Perhaps some had gone through that very wood, a few weeks ago.

Tears came into her eyes and she looked down to find her handkerchief. As she did so something moved on the slope below her and suddenly she saw three men standing there among the scrub.

Her heart gave a bound of fear, but then she saw their rough clothes and leggings; they were peasants. They were quite near, only yards below on the steep hillside. They were all looking at her, and then she saw they had guns slung over their shoulders, and her heart beat hard again.

She looked down at them and they looked up at her. The one in the middle was very tall, with thick black hair cropped to his ears, and there was a jagged red scar on the side of his face, noticeable even through the dark scrub of unshaven beard. That one certainly did look like a brigand, as the French called the rebels, Claudine thought.

And then this brigand, who was gazing up at her, suddenly smiled and kissed his hand to her.

Claudine stepped back, alarmed.

"Claudine!" called Seraphine's clear young voice below her. "Where are you? Claudine!"

The next moment a shot tore through the still air, ripping echoes from the valley.

The three men dropped down among the scrub and started crawling away down the hill.

It was none of them who had fired the shot. Claudine looked the other way and soon picked out dark moving shapes, and the flash of tricolour badges. A company of French soldiers were beating their way along the hillside. They had evidently caught sight of the rebel peasants and were now in pursuit of them, but were going carefully because they had seen that they too were armed.

Seraphine ran up and caught Claudine round the waist. "What is it, Claudine? What's happening?"

"The French – after some of the rebels," said Claudine, searching the hillside with her eyes. For a few moments she could not see the three men, so well had they disappeared into the rough country. But after all, the slope was steep and the bushes not big, nor did they cover the ground. She saw one of the men crawling, heard shouts from the French, and another shot cracked out.

Then the French began to run forward in a straggling line; they had bayonets fixed on their muskets.

The three rebels, giving up the attempt to remain unobserved, leapt up and ran away headlong down the hill. It was so steep that the running was dangerous; they jumped, slid, stumbled and crashed on down towards the woods at the bottom where the little river ran, to join one of the many tributaries of the Moselle which drained the country eastward towards the Rhine.

"Why don't they stop and fire their own guns?" Seraphine said. She had seen the rifles slung on the men's backs.

"There are too many of the French – and too near," said Claudine. "It would take too long to stop and load and aim . . ."

For some moments the French too had been running and scrambling without firing, but now, as they came to a ridge, it looked as if the peasants were going to get safe into the woods. Orders were shouted and several men dropped, each on one knee, and took aim. It was a regular salvo of shots.

"Oh heavens, have they killed them?" Claudine cried, in an agony.

She could not see the rebels down below the ledge, for the ground fell too steeply there.

"There goes one – falling down," Seraphine said, with a gasp.

Claudine saw him too now, on the last bank that sloped to the stream. It was the black-haired man who had kissed his hand to her and by the way he was falling she thought he must be dead already, for his body slid and rolled and tumbled down the rough cliff, crashing through bracken and bramble, right down and into the river, disappearing with a splash into a long dark pool.

"Oh, God!" whispered Claudine, holding on to her sister.

The French cheered, but they did not attempt to go down that precipitous slope to the river. They moved sideways, evidently in pursuit of the other two men, and presently the whole hunt vanished beyond a bluff.

The two girls stood staring down in horror at the river. They were too shocked by this sudden disaster to move. It was one thing to hear about the rebels being hunted down, even though they had felt sorry for them; it was another to see it happen. Only a few minutes before, that man had been alive, so much alive that, as Claudine could not forget, he had kissed his hand to her. And now he was dead.

It was Seraphine who said suddenly, in a shaky voice, "Claudine . . . isn't that his head?"

"His body, coming up," said Claudine, with a shudder, not looking.

"No, but it's his head . . . Claudine, it's moving. I believe he's still alive!"

That seemed almost worse to Claudine – a terribly
wounded man, still conscious. Shrinkingly she looked down
once more and saw a black head far below, and it was certainly moving. Carried by the stream, she thought at first,
but then she saw a brown hand splashing. The man was not
dead for he was trying to swim, or trying to get to the bank.
Then he was carried under some overhanging trees and they
could see him no more.

"Let's climb down and try to help him out," said
Seraphine impulsively.

"Seraphine, how can we get down there? You saw him
falling down! But we might go round, to where the river runs
out into the meadows . . . if there's time."

But as she spoke two things happened. A bell started
tolling behind them and the French soldiers came back
round the bluff. They had no prisoners with them, but
whether they had escaped or were dead, the girls did not
know.

Afraid that they might be seen and questioned they ran
back through the ruins and down the path towards the
château. The bell was ringing for the afternoon lesson, in any
case.

As they hurried, breathless, through the paths of the parterre, the bell suddenly stopped. And in the hall they found
two irate French officials.

"It is strictly forbidden to ring bells," one of them said
sternly. "All bells will be dismantled. Clock bells also. No
weapons, no alarm signals. It is by order."

"Dear me, I did not know that," Madame Bilsdorf, the
headmistress said, flustered by this sudden inspection.

"It is a new decree," said the unsmiling official. "From
Paris."

The two girls edged to the staircase and hurried up it to
take off their pelisses.

"They're frightened of us Luxembourgers," said
Seraphine exultantly. "They think we might rebel again, any
time."

"As if we could, when they've hunted down the men," said
Claudine.

In her mind's eye she kept seeing the black-haired man
with the scarred face falling helplessly down the cliff into the
river. But had he got away after all?

Seraphine was evidently thinking the same thing. "I hope that poor fellow wasn't drowned," she said.

"If he comes out in the meadows, they'll probably catch him," said her sister despondently.

"Mesdemoiselles – *citoyennes!*" called out one of the teachers, who never could remember the new rules of address. "To your places, *vite, vite!*"

It was almost impossible to attend to lessons that day.

CHAPTER
TWO

BY the evening everybody in the château knew about the hunting of the rebels; they were all talking about it – girls, teachers and servants. The servants had mostly been chosen by Monsieur de Trévires on the advice of Carl Kieffer, the former major-domo at Villerange, but a man who had not had much use for the aristocrats he had served. But some of the grooms and kitchen staff came from the village and one of the chambermaids, as the girls knew, though no one else did, had a brother who had taken to the woods.

Claudine and Seraphine found her in the bedroom they shared, taking off the counterpanes and bedewing them with tears.

"Lisel! What's the matter?" They ran to her, full of concern.

"Don't you know? They've shot him – everyone's talking of it."

Lisel did not know French; they spoke in dialect with her.

"Not your brother, Lisel?" Seraphine said, hesitating.

"No, not our Wenzel, thanks be to God," said the girl, wiping her eyes with her apron. "But his captain, his leader – the one the French call Le Cicatrisé – the Marked Man."

Claudine immediately remembered the scar she had seen on the man's cheek.

Seraphine, who did not know about that, asked if her brother had been with him.

"Yes, and he's so upset, poor Wenzel, he admired Gabry – that's what we call him – so much. Even though the rebellion has failed, he has kept them together, and rescued some of the conscripts." Lisel folded a counterpane and put it on a chair. "It was such bad luck. Wenzel and the other got away but Gabry was shot through the head – he's tall, an easy target."

"Has he got black hair?" asked Seraphine excitedly. "But

Lisel, he can't have been shot through the head. We saw him in the river. He wasn't dead."

She began to tell Lisel what they had seen. At first the girl seemed unable to take it in, but then she became very excited.

"Mademoiselle! This is wonderful! I must go and tell Wenzel at once. Oh if – Gabry is not dead, we may save him. But he will need help. Thank you, thank you, mademoiselle."

She ran away along the passage and they heard her feet clattering down wooden backstairs.

But Claudine said, "I daresay the French will find him first – have found him already."

"What a pessimist you are!" cried Seraphine. "If the French had found him, we should have heard by now. Wouldn't they bring him here, the nearest place? And they certainly would not be rambling about in the woods after it got dark."

All this was so true that Claudine felt more cheerful. Seraphine had a lot of common sense, in this taking after their mother rather than their father.

The next day they knew for certain that the rebel had not been caught, for someone brought a newspaper from Luxembourg – a mere sheet of official news, much of it copied from the Paris papers – in which there was a paragraph exulting in a violent end put to activities of "Le Cicatrisé" – the man with the scar. It was evident that the authorities considered him one of the most dangerous of the rebels, for there was much abuse of his murderous cunning in setting ambushes for companies of soldiers conducting recruits.

"Rescuing prisoners, that means," observed Seraphine, as the girls leaned over the table where the paper was laid.

"Seraphine!" exclaimed a serious girl who believed firmly in the ideals of the Revolution. "How can you say that – you, the daughter of Citoyen Trévires!"

Seraphine only laughed; she had not such reverence for her father's wisdom as Claudine had, perhaps because she was not such a reader of books as her sister. She knew she was safe from Lotte, who could hardly report the daughter of the school's founder for anti-revolutionary sentiments.

Of course she had said nothing of their belief that the rebel was not dead; they wondered what was happening, but did not see Lisel at all that day, or the next.

On the third day after the chase behind the ruins it rained hard and there was no possibility of going out during their free time in the afternoon. Seraphine was playing battledore and shuttlecock with an energetic friend and Claudine wandered away by herself, as she liked to do whenever she had the chance. She had always felt a great need of being alone for stretches of time.

The château of Villerange was larger than the school's needs, and one side of the building was left almost empty in winter, for it contained a gallery and ballroom and was difficult to heat. Claudine wandered through these empty halls, dreaming over the landscape pictures – none by the best artists, for the Erlen family had been chiefly interested in recording themselves for posterity. Claudine was already familiar with the array of earlier counts, in armour, or displaying decorations of the Austrian Empire, with their dark arrogant faces and curling lips – it was easy to believe in their reputation for evil temper.

"Robber Counts!" her father had said once. "That's what they were called in the middle ages and that's what they've remained, in effect – petty tyrants."

Claudine, although she had been fourteen before the French had driven the Austrian army out of Luxembourg, had never met the family of Villerange because of her father's republican views. But since being at school in their house she had heard many stories, especially about the late Count Bertrand d'Erlen, killed in the war of '92, who was said to have had such a violent temper that his servants went in terror of their lives. And Rémy Lefèvre had often told the girls how the old Count had had him beaten for calling him "tyrant" to his face.

Rémy was the son of Suzanne Kieffer, wife the major-domo; his father, François Lefèvre, her first husband, had died in a French prison where he had been thrown by the King's government, before the Revolution, for subversive writings. Monsieur de Trévires had educated Rémy and made him his secretary, so that he was very well known to Claudine; he was only a year older than herself.

Claudine wandered on, through the great ballroom, dim because the shutters were closed, making for a room beyond

it where there was a little harpsichord. In the summer she had
got someone to tune it, so that she could come and play and
sing there alone. It was so cold today that she wondered if her
fingers were not too chilly to attempt it.

The instrument was in the last of a series of small rooms,
used as card rooms, and opening from a wide passage. The
windows to the courtyard were unshuttered and so it was
quite light. Then, as Claudine passed the door of the middle
room she heard a noise that made her skin shiver. It was a
human groan.

She stood still, paralysed with horror.

Then she heard it again, and a sort of muddled muttering.
Someone was inside that room, groaning in pain.

Claudine braced herself. "It must be some poor servant
taken ill and unable to move," she told herself. "I must go in
and see."

Firmly she grasped the handle and opened the door.

She saw a man lying on the floor, covered with an old grey
blanket, and as she came in he turned his head with a start
and half raised himself on his elbow. He had a bandage round
his head but she recognised him at once. It was the man with
the scar, who had fallen down the cliff into the river.

Claudine stood staring at him in astonishment.

After a moment he said hoarsely, but with a hint of
amusement, "*Attendez, fantôme!*"

So he had recognised her too.

"Oh," said Claudine, "I am so glad you are not dead!"
Then, realising that a peasant might not know French, she
went on in the Luxembourger German. "But what are you
doing here? It must be dangerous for you."

"They brought me here," he said, lying down again, but
still looking at her. "It's Villerange, isn't it?"

She realised that he could not be fully aware of his situation; she saw now he was dazed and looked a bit feverish.

"Your head was hurt, after all," she said.

"Yes, like hell," he answered vaguely.

The next moment another man, whom she had never seen
before, came in by a second door. When he saw her he turned
quite pale. He was dressed like one of the outdoor servants,
in serviceable breeches and stockings, with a short jacket, not
a coat.

"Mademoiselle! You are one of the young ladies of the

school?" he said anxiously. "I thought none came into this wing in winter. You see my – my friend is resting here."

"She saw me on the hill, Norbert," said the man on the floor. "She knows that the French are out for my blood."

"The French think you are dead," said Claudine.

"Do they? Excellent!" he said.

Although he spoke in German, it was not as broad as the peasants talked.

Norbert had a bottle of wine in his hand. The man with the scar made a gesture towards it. "Come on, Norbert, give me a dose. I need it."

Norbert was looking anxiously at Claudine. "Mademoiselle, you won't give him away? We had to bring him indoors somewhere. This was the nearest place – he would not go to Wenzel's parents for fear of reprisals if he was found there. I did not want to leave him alone, but it is difficult . . ."

"Norbert! Stop chattering," said the man with the scar, "and give me that good medicine."

"Now, listen, Monsieur Gabry, I don't think you should have much," said Norbert, but he knelt down and helped his patient to sit up and drink the wine from a metal cup.

Claudine stood watching. She saw that this Gabry's friends had made a bed for him on the floor with cushions and blankets. A bowl of water with another bloodstained bandage in it, and a guttered candle in an earthenware holder showed that he must have been there at least one night.

The wine seemed to put new life into Gabry. Claudine found he was looking at her again. He had green eyes, green hazel, bright and keen. He was a remarkable looking man, in spite of his present pallor and unshaven black chin, even in spite of the jagged red scar which disfigured one side of his face. He had black arching brows, a hooked nose and a hard jaw line. He looked about thirty.

"What made you come here, *fantôme*?" he said. "Isn't it cold, even for a ghost, in these empty rooms?"

"I like being alone," said Claudine. "I came to play on the harpsichord – there's one in the next room."

"Do you often do that, mademoiselle?" asked Norbert. "They know you do it?"

He was a solidly built man, fairly tall, with a heavy, earnest face and looked about the same age as the other. His brown hair grew in a thick thatch, forward on his head.

"Yes, why?" Claudine said.

"Mademoiselle, if you could but stay here while I go and find him some clothes," said Norbert. "It would be far easier to hide him if he were not in those dirty torn things which just proclaim him a rebel."

"But how can you get any?" said Claudine, surprised. "You'll never find your way about this big house – I still get lost myself sometimes, and I've been here more than two years."

Norbert looked taken aback. He glanced at the man on the floor, who was lying there listening.

"Norbert knows this house well," said Gabry. "He worked here as a servant when the old Count was alive."

"Did you really?" said Claudine, interested. "Wasn't he a very wicked man? Everyone says so."

Gabry laughed and Norbert said, "Not wicked, mademoiselle – just very quick-tempered. But now, will you stay and keep watch?"

"But what shall I do if someone comes?" Claudine asked nervously.

Norbert took the key from the inside of the door and put it in the lock on the outside. "If you hear anyone coming, just lock the door and take the key," he said. "If by mischance the person is determined to get in, he can do so by going through the next room, but by that time Monsieur Gabry could get out of the other. He can move, he only needs a little longer than usual to do it."

"Very well, I'll watch," said Claudine.

Norbert thanked her and started off at once.

"Hey, Norbert!" cried Gabry. "How do you think I am going to get up and run when you've taken half my clothes away? A fine thing if I'm to run round a girl's school in my shirt!"

Norbert grinned. "I'd forgotten that!" he said. "They aren't dry yet, your breeches, I'm afraid, but better than nothing! Mademoiselle, you had better go and play on that little clavier next door till we are ready."

Claudine went into the adjoining card room and played, softly, on the harpsichord, already listening for unwanted footsteps. She heard the two men laughing next door and the grunts and muffled oaths of the patient as he was dressed. Even apart from his head wound, he must be stiff and sore after falling down the hillside, she thought.

When Norbert put his head round the door to say they were ready she rose hastily. "Don't be long, will you? I have only about half an hour more free time," she said.

Norbert hurried away and Claudine went into the passage and sat down on a window seat. Here she could see each way, and right through the ballroom. She could also see the rebel leader in the room opposite; he was now sitting propped up against the wall, on top of his makeshift bed.

"How charming you look there, *fantôme*," he said in French.

"Oh – you speak French?" she said in surprise.

"Yes, I've lived up in the Walloon country," he said. "I've been a soldier too."

"I thought you didn't seem like a peasant," said Claudine. "Lisel said you were one of their leaders – she cried when she thought you were dead."

"Lisel is a good girl," said Gabry. "She brought me some fine soup last night, and now she has got us this wine. I hope she won't get into trouble – nor you, either, mademoiselle, for helping one of the enemies of the people." He smiled as he repeated this catch phrase of the revolutionaries.

"I can't understand how you weren't killed – they said you were shot through the head, in the paper," said Claudine.

Gabry laughed. "Of course they liked to think it was such a good shot," he said. "But Norbert tells me the bullet has only grazed my scalp. I can't remember a thing. I must have hit my head when I fell down. I have a vague memory of being in the river and somehow crawling out under the trees. Wenzel and Norbert found me, the same night, I think – Wenzel's sister told him where to look – Lisel, that is."

"Yes, and we told her," said Claudine. "Seraphine, my sister, told her we had seen you swimming – well, afloat."

"Did you?" he said. "So then I owe a lot to you. Seraphine – and your name, what's that?"

Claudine told him her Christian name but no more.

"Claudine – that's pretty," he said.

"Does your head hurt?" she asked.

"Not much now," said Gabry.

"But you were groaning – that's why I came in."

"Was I? In my sleep, then," he said. "I can't move without discovering just how many muscles got pulled and bones knocked – but I'm lucky, as nothing seems to be broken. I'll be all right in a day or two. Norbert was scared because I was silly at first – concussed, I suppose."

In spite of the easy way he spoke Claudine soon realised that talking was tiring him and she said he ought to stay quiet and rest.

"Sing me a lullaby, then," he suggested. "I heard you singing in the ruins, like a blackbird – one of our old ballads."

Claudine was much too shy to sing it to him direct but she managed to walk up and down the passage, softly singing over old songs, some in the German dialect, some in French, until Norbert came back.

He had clothes over his arm, shoes in one hand and a jug of hot water and a razor in the other.

"Ah!" said Gabry. "Norbert is determined I shan't look like a brigand any more. Next time I see you, mademoiselle, you won't recognise me."

"Is there anything else I can do?" asked Claudine, hovering in the doorway.

"Yes – come back tomorrow," said Gabry hopefully.

"Mademoiselle, could you do that?" Norbert asked. "I would like to get him upstairs – hardly anyone is sleeping in this wing. It would be a help if you could act again as a scout for us."

"I'll come if I possibly can," said Claudine.

"And you'll tell no one, mademoiselle?" said Norbert anxiously. "You see, if this one is found, they will most certainly shoot him, or send him to the guillotine."

"I won't tell anyone – except, may I tell my sister? She would make a better scout than me, I believe, and she admires the rebels." ·

"As long as she can keep her mouth shut," said Norbert.

Claudine smiled and said, "She will, if I explain how dangerous it is."

As she turned, Gabry called out, *"Adieu, fantôme!"*

Claudine laughed as she walked away. She thought herself a remarkably solid ghost, but the joke amused her.

CHAPTER
THREE

SERAPHINE was thrilled to hear that the rebel leader was hiding in the castle and wanted to go and see him at once, although, when she heard the news they were undressing for bed and she was standing in her shift, barefooted. Eagerly she asked, "What is he like?"

"He's not an ordinary peasant," said Claudine. "He's been a soldier."

"That's why he makes a good leader, I expect," said Seraphine. "I do hope he stays here for days. I shall save my apple for him. I wish it was tomorrow."

And for her it very soon was, for she fell asleep quickly.

Claudine was more than usually dreamy at lesson time next day; she was thinking about her rebel. She wanted to see him again, and yet there was something hard and rough about him which she found indefinably alarming.

And then, after dinner, difficulties began to multiply.

In the first place, Mademoiselle Charpentier insisted that they should go outside.

"What, such a fine day, and you don't want to go out?" she said. "That is unlike the daughters of dear Monsieur de Trévires!"

Mademoiselle Charpentier, a desiccated old woman nearing fifty, cherished an ardent admiration for Gautier de Trévires, whom she regarded as a kind of saint of republicanism.

"Never mind, we can get in at the side door, near the room where your harpsichord is," whispered the resourceful Seraphine.

And then Rémy Lefèvre, their father's young secretary, arrived with a letter, and was sent to take it to them as they walked sedately in the parterre.

Rémy walked eagerly towards the girls. He had been a clever, clumsy boy when they first met him, but now he was a young man, sturdily built, with thick brown hair which would hang in a fringe above his eyes, however often he pushed it back. Those eyes were clear blue in his brown face. Rémy's feelings were strong and he was not good at controlling them. Perhaps because of his chequered childhood he was inclined to be on the defensive, suspicious of other people's intentions and very serious about his own. For this Seraphine teased him mercilessly.

"Oh Rémy, do laugh!" she would say. "You look as solemn as a bear!"

When he did laugh, it changed his whole face; but it was a rare thing for Rémy to laugh.

Every since he was about thirteen Rémy had been falling madly in love with girls far above him in station and so beautiful that he dared not approach them. Just now it was Claudine. And although he had never said anything of his hopeless passion, the sisters were well aware of it.

"Is it hopeless?" Seraphine had once asked Claudine, wickedly. "Don't you love him even one little bit?"

"Love Rémy? Don't be silly, Seraphine," said Claudine.

But she was too kind-hearted to be anything but gentle to him, so that he continued to adore without letting himself believe it altogether hopeless. After all, in this brave new republican world, were not all men equal?

Madame de Trévires, who regarded Rémy as belonging to a lower social order in spite of his writing father martyred by the men of the *ancien régime,* because his mother was only a member of a musician's family, thought her husband unwise to encourage Rémy's familiarity with their daughter. But Monsieur de Trévires thought of the girls as mere children still.

"*Citoyennes!*" said Rémy, coming up with his hat under his arm. "You both look very well and charming."

He handed over the letter but plainly had no intention of going away. He paced beside them while the letter, which was quite short, was read first by one sister and then the other. It was merely about the arrangements for taking them home for the few days which had once been the Christmas holidays. But now that Christmas had been abolished, it was called the midwinter vacation.

"Tell Papa we shall be ready on the day he names, Rémy, please," said Claudine. She was longing for him to go, but did not how to get rid of him without hurting his feelings.

"I suppose you rode over?" Seraphine said. "Won't you have to start soon if you're to get home by dark?"

"I have to give my poor beast a rest," said Rémy cheerfully. "Besides, it's a long time since I saw you. I came now on purpose, because I know you are free in the afternoon."

Of course he would do that, thought Claudine, at her wit's end.

Presently, as they walked along the paths, he spoke of the shooting of the rebel known as Le Cicatrisé. "I was horrified when I heard it had happened here," he said. "I know your kind heart, Citoyenne Claudine."

"I should have thought you would be pleased, Rémy – one less to fight for the aristocrats," said Seraphine, wickedly.

"Well, one need not be sorry for this man," Rémy said. "He wasn't a simple peasant but a soldier – an Austrian, some people say, and a savage, treacherous sort of man."

"How do you know that?" Seraphine asked, while Claudine simply stared at him with her large pensive grey eyes.

"We had two French officers at Hautefontaine yesterday," said Rémy, "and they told us some of his exploits. Even Madame your mother said she would prefer that such men should not be at large."

Seraphine at once wanted to hear these tales but Rémy shook his head, saying, "I couldn't tell you," so that Claudine began to imagine all kinds of horrors. At last, teased by Seraphine, he told of an ambush and massacre of French soldiers escorting recruits to Luxembourg. Only a few had escaped to tell the tale and that was how it became known that Le Cicatrisé had directed the raid – they had seen him in action.

As Claudine listened she felt that the man she had seen would be capable of carrying out that bloody business. She sighed.

"I should not have told you," said Rémy anxiously. "It has upset you, Citoyenne."

"It is war," she answered, "and we are still living in a war, even though that treaty was made."

"Your father does not think that treaty will last much longer," said Rémy, and began to talk about a letter from a republican friend beyond the Rhine.

Time was passing and Claudine thought of the rebel Gabry lying wounded in the little card room, and his faithful Norbert, waiting and watching for her. At last she looked at Seraphine in desperation. "I think I'll have to go in," she said. "My headache is worse."

"That's right," said her sister at once. "Why don't you go in by that little side door? I will see Rémy has some refreshment before he goes."

And although Rémy showed signs of wanting to escort Claudine indoors, Seraphine steered him firmly away towards the main entrance and the visitors' parlour, to ply him with cake and wine.

Claudine slipped in at the small door, which had been put at the end of the ballroom wing, just beyond the card rooms. It led into a small lobby from which rose some narrow stairs, boxed in and steep; Claudine had often wondered why they were there.

Norbert was standing in the doorway of the room where he had hidden Gabry. "Mademoiselle, I saw you in the garden," he said. "Is it safe? That young man won't come looking for you?"

"No, no, he thinks I'm going to bed with a headache," said Claudine. "Now, what do you want me to do?"

"Please, mademoiselle, to go up those stairs and keep watch at the top, so that we do not by mischance walk into somebody's arms."

Claudine nodded and hurried up the dark stairs. On the landing it was very quiet. All the doors in the passage up here were shut. These were first floor rooms, stately chambers for guests, not at present in use. The air smelt musty and there was a thin rim of dust on the window sills.

"It's all right," Claudine called softly down.

Presently she heard the two men coming up. She realised now why her help was needed; the wounded rebel could not have got up the stairs alone. All Norbert's attention was taken up in assisting him. It was a slow, stumbling climb, both men breathing heavily with the strain. And when they reached the top, Gabry's face had gone a yellowish pale colour.

Claudine backed into the passage, looking and listening, but there was no one about. Norbert had evidently decided already which room to use and they moved towards it, shuffling along, Gabry balancing himself with one hand against the wall.

Claudine opened the door for them; the key was in the lock. There was a big fourposter bed in the room but no beclothes. The shutters were up and it was rather dim, at once chill and airless. But there was less danger up here that they would be seen from outside the house.

Gabry sat down on the bedstead and held on to the post.

"I'll go and bring the blankets," Norbert said, and hurried off.

"Bring up the wine first!" Gabry called after him, but softly.

Claudine came closer. "You seem worse than yesterday," she said, nervously.

"I'm not," he answered. "Climbing is hard, that's all."

"Let me look at your head," said Claudine. "We had wounded men at Hautefontaine in the war and my mother taught me a lot."

"Hautefontaine?" he repeated, opening his eyes properly and giving her a keen look. "Where – Citoyen Trévires lives?"

"Yes, he's my father, but I shan't tell him about you."

Gabry stared at her for a moment and then began to chuckle.

"The republican's daughter!" he said. "Who would have thought it?"

Norbert came up, carrying the bottle of wine, a blanket and a water can.

"Mademoiselle proposes to examine my head," said Gabry. "Perhaps to decide the best way of cutting it off, for she is the child of old Trévires of Hautefontaine, the – what shall I call him? Not the Robespierre of Luxembourg, but perhaps the Mirabeau."

Norbert looked thoroughly alarmed, even when Claudine assured him her father need know nothing. But she convinced him at last, both of her goodwill and of her ability to dress wounds, and presently she was allowed to unwind the bandage from the rebel's head. His black hair, matted with blood, had been roughly cut away round the scalp wound.

Claudine had spoken the truth; she was quite an efficient nurse. She clipped away more hair, bathed the wound, and bound it up more neatly than Norbert had done.

Gabry, who had taken a swig of the wine before she began, now took another and remarked, "You are a cool hand, Mademoiselle de Trévires!"

Norbert had meanwhile been carrying up the rest of the gear. He left the door open, to admit light and air.

Claudine only now became aware of how different her patient was looking from when she had first seen him. He was wearing the same sort of clothes as Norbert, plain homespun, worsted stockings and flat shoes, with a handkerchief loosely knotted round his neck, but this and his coarse linen shirt were clean and now that he was shaven he looked even less like a peasant. Claudine even felt she had seen him before; there was something familiar about the hard lines of those hawklike features and curling lip – though the odd twist when he smiled was partly due to the scar which had pulled up the skin on the left side.

He was smiling now, and at her, she thought, suddenly uncomfortable, because she knew she had been staring at him.

"So Villerange is a school for girls," he said, and this seemed to amuse him. "I had not realised that; I haven't been back in this part of the country for some time. Well! At least this fate has saved it from those revolutionary thieves. But I must not say that to you, the daughter of a well-known republican."

"My father is not a thief," said Claudine, indignantly. "The castle belongs to the French government. The Count who owned it is fighting with the enemy, so his property is forfeit."

"The enemy? But the Emperor is our sovereign in Luxembourg," said Gabry. "The French are invaders. They have no right here."

"I mean that the Count is an enemy of the Republic," said Claudine seriously. "My father is loyal to the *idea* of the Republic, and at present that is represented by France."

Gabry regarded her still with a smiling face; his hazel green eyes bright with amusement. He had recovered from his climb; the colour had come back to his skin.

"You are a true daughter of the Revolution!" he said. "But then why do you assist one of its enemies? For so I am, and not an inactive one."

"I hate all the fighting and killing," said Claudine. "But I think the aristocrats got what they deserved, especially in France. Even here some were bad men – these counts of Villerange, for instance. But if you come from another part of the country, you may not know about them."

"Oh, everybody has heard of those robber counts," said Gabry. "But were they still robbing till yesterday? Surely only living on the ill-gotten gains of their ancestors?"

"Isn't that almost as bad?" said Claudine. "But indeed the Erlens have all been fierce and cruel. The old Count beat his servants."

"He beat his sons too," said Gabry. "So Norbert tells me."

"But it didn't make them any better," said Claudine.

"No?" He looked at her, smiling. "How did you discover that, Mademoiselle Claudine?"

"Because my father has told me how wild the young Counts were," she said. "Especially the eldest one. Do you know, when he was only a boy he lamed his cousin for life, pushing him off a wall? I know that's true, because he's our cousin too, on his mother's side: Thierry de Ravanger of Isenbourg. He's been in England four years now, married to an English girl – but I remember him quite well."

The rebel did not say anything, but the smile had gone out of his face.

"Father says the Erlens were good for nothing but fighting," said Claudine.

"I've no doubt he is right," said Gabry, the gleam returning to his green eyes. "I don't wish to defend the Counts of Villerange, Mademoiselle, from your just censure. But nor do I want Frenchmen dictating to us how to live and since they hold us down by force I think we are justified in fighting back."

"Even with ambush and massacre?" Claudine said. She had not meant to get into argument with him but Rémy's story was fresh in her mind.

"They were soldiers, and armed," said Gabry. "Better armed than we were, with our old muskets and flails." He looked her straight in the eye. "Mademoiselle, I have done nothing I am ashamed to have done."

Claudine found that she could not disbelieve him; whatever she might feel about such violent warfare, he thought it fair. His eyes were clear and honest, his voice had a ring of truth.

She sighed, but could find nothing to say. There was a moment of silence between them. Gabry still sitting on the bed, Claudine standing opposite.

Far off, Claudine heard a tiny insistent sound. One of the teachers was ringing a handbell, the only bell now allowed in the school.

"Oh, I must go," she said. "I can hear the bell for lessons."

Gabry smiled again. "Do not look so sad, my dear," he said, as if he were speaking to a child. "If we choose to fight for freedom in Luxembourg, it is not your fault when men get killed, on either side. Continue to be the good angel of the wounded, of both sides!" Then he laughed. "But there are no angels in the republican world, are there? So be one of those beautiful personifications the artists are so fond of drawing: Concordia, Clemencia – the classical virtues."

Claudine found herself smiling back as she said a quick farewell. She ran off, down the twisting stairs, along the passage and through the ballroom, and the gallery, hurrying past the portraits of the proud black-haired Erlens, petty tyrants of the time that was gone.

CHAPTER
FOUR

THE next day, to Claudine's surprise, the carriage arrived from Hautefontaine with orders to take her and Seraphine home – "for your birthday, mademoiselle," said the old coachman.

Claudine had never been home for her birthday before and only yesterday her father had written making arrangements for Christmas, still some weeks away, without any mention of an earlier visit.

The headmistress was equally surprised, though Monsieur de Trévires had written her a brief note, saying that he would only keep her daughters two nights.

"It was a sudden wish of your mother's," she told the girls.

They did not think that much of their mother, whose affection was constant but not at all demonstrative.

Because they had to leave directly after the early school dinner Claudine had no opportunity to go and see the rebels and she was afraid they would think she had abandoned them. But there was nothing to be done. Seraphine, when they were alone in the family coach, bumping over the cross-country roads, said gloomily, "And now I daresay I shall not see the rebels at all. They will be gone when we get back."

"They don't look like rebels any more," Claudine said. "More like the men who clean the shoes. Except . . ." she hesitated, seeing in her mind's eye that incisive eagle profile of Gabry's.

"Except what?" Seraphine was looking at her with bright inquisitive eyes.

"Well, he doesn't look like a servant – the one called Gabry," said her sister. "I suppose it's because he was a soldier."

Hautefontaine lay east and slightly north of the Luxembourg city, in the beechwoods. Claudine's birthday, tomorrow, was the twenty-first of November, and the beautiful trees were almost bare, standing in the coppery drifts of their leaves, though some still clung to the twigs in fluttering sprays.

A long drive ran curving round a gentle slope towards the house which stood in a shallow vale among the wooded hills. It was not a great place like the château of Villerange, but an old country house, built in the seventeenth century on the site of one much older. The kitchens and outbuildings were even more ancient.

Claudine loved Hautefontaine passionately, every golden grey stone of it, every corner of the gardens, all the woods around and the waterfall up the valley from which it derived its name. She had never been away from it except to visit relations in Luxembourg and to the school at Villerange. Seraphine was longing to travel, to see Paris and Rome, but Claudine would have been content just to imagine these great cities, as she listened to her father telling of them, for he had travelled much in his youth.

"It's lovely to come home before all the leaves have gone," she said now.

It was late in the afternoon and the light was already fading as they descended from the carriage. As they went into the hall they heard music – someone was playing the pianoforte which Madame de Trévires had bought just before the war; she was delighted to have secured this latest instrument of civilisation before such things became, for the time being, unobtainable.

Claudine stopped, poised, on the threshold.

"But *who* is that playing?" she whispered.

None of them could play like that.

Seraphine was already tiptoeing towards the open door of the drawing room and Claudine went after her, looking over her head, for she was a good deal taller.

No one was in the room but the thin man in a blue coat who was sitting there playing in the dusk, evidently knowing by heart the sonata he played, which was by Mozart. The sisters could see his dark head, the hair falling forward in thick locks, which he shook back suddenly.

Then he saw them in the doorway, stopped playing and got up.

"Why, it is my little *cousines*, is it not?" he said, coming towards them quickly but with an uneven, limping walk.

"It is Cousin Thierry!" cried Claudine.

"From England!" said Seraphine, staring.

"Hush!" he said, putting a finger to his lips. "That's just why you have been brought home now – to learn not to recognise me so well!"

Both of them realised then that their cousin, who was the Count of Isenbourg, a castle further north, would be regarded by the occupying French as a proscribed aristocrat, one of the hated *émigrés* who had joined France's enemies. Although the situation was really different in Luxembourg, since that duchy had long been part of the Holy Roman Empire, the French insisted that it was rightfully part of France, and treated its landowners as they treated their own.

The next moment Madame de Trévires came hastening downstairs. She was a small woman, growing plump in middle age, but always neat and well dressed.

"I suppose my silly girls have been shrieking your name already," she said. "However, you are safe enough here, Thierry – as safe as you would be in your own Isenbourg, where your people are all loyal as can be. I daresay Gautier would contradict me, on principle, but it is true, nevertheless."

Thierry de Ravanger laughed. He had a wide mouth, which made deep creases in his thin face when he smiled. His eyelids were heavy, often hooding his grey eyes, hiding their expression. He was a year or so over thirty and not much changed since they had last seen him, four years ago, but in the interval the girls had grown up and they saw him now with different eyes. But he had always been a favourite visitor, bringing his two young half-brothers, or sometimes carrying them off to stay at Isenbourg, one of the most romantic castles of the country, standing up on a crag in a loop of the river Sûre.

The girls went upstairs to change their dress and ate a second dinner before they were able to hear why their cousin had made this sudden appearance among them. After the meal the candles were lit in the drawing room, the shutters and doors were closed, and they sat together round the fire.

"Thierry arrived yesterday, while Rémy Lefèvre was at Villerange," said Madame de Trévires. "So we could not let you know. He has false papers, made out under an assumed name, so we must not any longer call him by his own. I do not believe anyone who knows him would willingly give him away, but it might happen by accident."

"We won't do it," said Seraphine. "What are you calling yourself, Cousin?"

"Henri Théry," he replied. "I hope you will find Citoyen Théry as easy to say as Cousin Thierry."

"I think you invented that name to help my silly girls remember it," said his aunt, smiling.

"Well, I knew I must come here, and did not know they were at school," he said. "I did not know Villerange was turned into a school! It seems incongruous, when one thinks of the Erlens."

"Have you seen them lately?" Madame de Trévires asked.

"No – Gabriel went off to Vienna soon after my marriage," said Thierry, "and Dominique was in Italy, being defeated by General Bonaparte, whom he seems to admire. I don't know what they have been doing since peace was made."

Monsieur de Trévires began to talk of the political situation, but his wife swiftly brought the conversation back to personal affairs.

"Thierry has come to help your Uncle Xavier," she told her daughters.

"Actually I came to mèet him at the Rhine and take him to England," said Thierry. "But when I heard he was taken, I felt I had to come on here."

"Taken?" cried Seraphine. "Is Uncle Xavier a prisoner?"

"Yes," said her mother sadly. "The French captured him on his way and we do not know where they have imprisoned him."

Her brother, Xavier de Lamerle, was a priest; ever since the girls could remember they had visited him in Luxembourg and he had come for holidays at Hautefontaine, a thin pale man in black, with whom their father had tried to argue, while he generally laughed and refused to answer. He was not a parish priest but a scholarly Abbé, who said Mass every day for a convent but otherwise spent his time in libraries. It was difficult to think of anyone less dangerous to society but to the revolutionaries all priests were suspect and Xavier de Lamerle was one of the many who had refused to take the oath to the republican constitution. He was therefore proscribed and as much in danger as any aristocrat.

"Surely they won't guillotine Uncle Xavier?" said Seraphine, horrified.

"But Xavier is not strong," said Madame de Trévires. "He is so thin, and coughs so much. If they put him underground, as they did the poor peasants, that would kill him as surely as the guillotine."

"Well, I will find out where he is," said Monsieur de Trévires. "That at least I can do. Whether I can secure his release is another thing, for the Commissaire seems to care more for French power than republican ideals."

Next morning Madame de Trévires took her daughters to mass in the village for the feast of Notre Dame and Thierry went with them. The church was half empty, for many of the villagers stayed away because the priest had taken the constitutional oath. Probably they were celebrating the mass with a priest in hiding, somewhere in the woods. But because Madame de Trévires felt that she should not endanger her husband's reputation as a good republican, she put up with the constitutional priest, even though her brother was one of those who refused compromise with avowed atheists.

On the way home Thierry wanted to walk back by the waterfall which gave Hautefontaine its name, and the two girls were put down with him. The path wound through the woods and here it was safe to ask him about England. They both remembered Petronella, the copperheaded English girl who had visited her aunt, Thierry's stepmother, just before the war began in 1792. Apparently they were all living together now in a small house at Brompton, a village on the outskirts of London.

"It is just not too far to walk to my work from there, if I start in good time," said Thierry.

"Your work?" said Seraphine in surprise. "What work can you do, Cousin Thierry?"

Thierry laughed. "You may well ask!" he said. "But I sell pianofortes – I demonstrate their qualities to the customers."

"You sell things in a shop!" cried Seraphine, astonished. "You, the Count of Isenbourg!"

"I am very glad to have this regular job, I can tell you that," said Thierry. "Sometimes I play for evening entertainments too. Even so, it is quite difficult to keep our household going."

Claudine asked about his brothers; the elder, Jofried, was almost a year older than herself. Apparently friends had bought him a commission in the British army.

"He looks very fine in his uniform," said Thierry. "He's grown big and tall – taller than I am."

Thierry was not small, but his height was only moderate. He was thin but wiry, quite strong in spite of his lame leg. He had his left shoes and boots built up, but his walking was a little awkward nevertheless.

The waterfall fell between high rocks into a deep pool, where they stood some time, fascinated by the crystal stream and the showering of water on water.

As they turned away Thierry said he wondered if Petronella had yet got the letter he had written before crossing the Rhine.

"Won't she be very anxious?" Claudine said.

"I made it sound as safe as I could," said Thierry. "And so far it has certainly been easy. After all, I don't look quite the noble aristocrat, do I?"

It was true; he did not. He was a quiet, unassuming person, not striking in appearance, and his sober dress was suited to some minor profession. His lameness, too, made him seem harmless.

As they came from the woodland path into the gardens of the house a short stocky man, with grey hair sticking up on his square head, came hurrying towards them.

"Seigneur, some French officers have called – Monsieur de Trévires told me to warn you," he said, in evident alarm. "Should you not retreat into the woods?"

"What sort of officers, Willibrord?" asked Thierry. "Senior?"

"Oh no, Seigneur, only a couple of lieutenants. One is a friend of that young Rémy Lefèvre, who seems to have done so well for himself since you sent him to Monsieur de Trévires."

Willibrord was Thierry's personal servant and had followed him through thick and thin. He was named after the Anglo-Saxon apostle of Luxembourg who had come from Northumbria in the seventh century and lay buried at Echternach, not far away.

"Rémy is given to making awkward friends," observed Thierry. "But he won't give me away."

"He'd better not," growled Willibrord, "considering all you have done for him. But you, mesdemoiselles, please remember not to refer to the Seigneur as your own Cousin Thierry."

Seraphine, giggling, promised to call him Citoyen Théry.

"Don't notice me at all," said Thierry. "I am an inferior being and Monsieur de Trévires is thinking of employing me to teach music in his school."

"Oh, I wish you would!" cried Seraphine. "I am sure you would make it more interesting than Madame Kieffer does – Rémy's mother."

Thierry laughed and went into the house by the back way, with Willibrord. Seraphine told her sister that one of the things he intended to do in Luxembourg was to find out what had happened to Willibrord's son, left behind on their flight to England four years ago, and now just of conscript age.

"So they want to go over to Isenbourg to find out."

"But everyone at Isenbourg will recognise Thierry!" said Claudine.

"And if they do?" said Seraphine. "Not one would give him away! *He* was not a tyrant, like the Counts of Villerange."

They went into the house and found the young French officers in the drawing room. Rémy's friend, Jules Desroux, they already knew, for his sister Annette was at school; they were French, from just across the old border in Lorraine. Desroux was good looking and immediately began to pay compliments to Claudine, which embarrassed her, especially as it always stirred Rémy's latent jealousy. Rémy was there too, looking a little anxious, Claudine thought. But when Thierry came in, nobody paid much attention to him. The young officers took him for one of Monsieur de Trévires' many earnest followers, and Thierry looked so deferential when their father spoke that the girls wanted to giggle.

The other lieutenant was older than Desroux, a stocky young man with a thrusting chin and uncouth manners; his name was Gaston Ferrand, and he had obviously won his way since the revolution.

The two officers drank rather too much wine at dinner and Ferrand became progressively louder and more revolutionary in his sentiments, boasting of recent exploits against the peasant rebels.

"Poor fools," said Jules Desroux. "I am sorry for them, led by their priests and seigneurs. It is men like them we came to liberate – and yet they prefer their chains!"

"They would learn their lesson sooner if they were not treated like conquered enemies," observed Monsieur de Trévires. "You Frenchmen are patriotic; you ought to understand the same feeling among German-speaking peoples."

"The Austrians have been corrupting them," said Gaston Ferrand in his harsh downright voice. "This country is full of agents – I believe Le Cicatrisé is one. But I wish he had been caught, not shot. To send a man like that to the guillotine would make a real example and put fear into the rest. Executing squareheads impresses nobody."

"But if he was Austrian, would it not have made trouble with Austria to execute him?" asked Monsieur de Trévires. "We are at peace with Austria now – officially."

"The peace won't last long now," said Gaston Ferrand. "And Vienna is a long way off. Slicing a man's head is quick work – by the time they heard of it we might be at war again."

"Messieurs, keep this sort of talk till we have left the table," said Madame de Trévires, noticing how pale Claudine had gone.

"The women of Paris have stronger nerves," said Ferrand. "They used to sit by the guillotine and cheer when the heads fell – heads of the enemies of the people."

Claudine jumped up and hurried out of the room. Her mother, in extreme displeasure, rose and followed her, summoning Seraphine with a glance.

The lieutenant thought it politic to remove his friend and the two officers left soon afterwards.

As they went to bed, Seraphine said gleefully, "He little knew Le Cicatrisé was alive, and convalescing in our school!"

But Claudine could only think of what might happen to the rebel leader if he were discovered.

CHAPTER
FIVE

ON the afternoon of the day after her return to school
Claudine went to look for the rebels and Seraphine went with
her. They first tried to get in at the door by the stairs, but it
was locked. So they slipped into the house again by the side
door which the girls all used, going into and out of the
garden, where there was a lobby for their cloaks and outdoor
shoes. This meant that they had to walk the length of the
gallery and ballroom. The card rooms at the end were all
empty now, though Seraphine looked inside, trying to
imagine what it had been like for Claudine to find the
wounded rebel on the floor.

The next setback was the discovery that the door at the
bottom of the boxed-in stairs was locked too.

"They must have gone," said Claudine. "Or have been
caught."

"We should have heard if they had been caught!"
Seraphine said. "The whole school would have buzzed with
the news. Let's go up the back stairs."

They turned the corner into that part of the castle which
housed the kitchens and offices and climbed the wooden
stairs to the landing, walking along the passage. At the head
of the little side stairs was another door, locked too.

After trying the handle they walked on and Claudine saw a
key in the lock of the bedroom where she had last seen Gabry
and Norbert. Without much hope now, she turned it and
opened the door.

The room was as empty as it had been when she first
entered it, the shutters still closed, the bed bare of blankets
and covered with unbleached linen. It again smelt airless in
there.

"Gone," said Seraphine, disappointed.

"He must be better then," said Claudine, shutting the
door again.

As they walked back along the passage, turning the corner

they almost ran into Lisel, who was carrying a covered pail. She gasped and then said in relief, "Oh, it's only you!"

"Lisel, what's happened? Have they gone?" Claudine asked.

"Oh no, mademoiselle, just moved to another room," said Lisel, "I was bringing their dinner, and you gave me such a fright!"

"Where are they now, then?"

To their surprise, Lisel giggled. "They are in the old Count's hunting room," she said.

"His what?" said Seraphine, her mouth dropping open.

Still giggling, Lisel said, "That's what they call it. It seems he was very fond of hunting, and when Madame la Comtesse was in such poor health, he did not want to disturb her by getting up early, so he had this side stair made and sometimes slept in this room."

"But why were the stairs boxed in?" Seraphine asked. "Why the locked doors?"

"Well, mesdemoiselles, perhaps I should not tell you what people say about the old Count – after all, he is dead now."

This was too much for the girls' curiosity.

"Oh, Lisel, you must tell us!" cried Seraphine.

"It's only that he used to go after women in the village," said Lisel. "And when he got older he found it more convenient to have his favourite up here. The door to the room is inside the staircase. So it makes a good hiding place."

"Then why didn't they go there straight away?" Claudine asked.

"Because Norbert could not get hold of the keys," said Lisel. "It was a tricky job, that – but he's persistent, is Norbert." She giggled again.

Down below in the courtyard a handbell began to sound, energetically rung by one of the teachers.

"Oh dear! And now we have not seen them!" cried Seraphine, in disappointment.

"I'll tell them you are back," said Lisel. "I don't think they'll be here much longer. Monsieur Gabry is much better. He says he will go out in the garden first, when there's no one about, and then they'll be away to the woods again."

The handbell jingled insistently below and the girls had to

hurry, if they were not to be seen coming from the wrong direction and questioned. They hurried down the back-stairs, ran through the ballroom and gallery, and joined in with the tail of the group coming into the lobby from the garden.

"What a wicked old man the last Count must have been!" said Seraphine. "He looks it, in his picture."

"Which is his picture?" Claudine asked.

"Don't you know? It's at this end of the gallery. He's wearing a grand uniform with decorations and standing by his horse with his sword drawn. He's got a wig, of course, but his eyebrows are black. He looks very fierce."

"No talking, Citoyennes," said Mademoiselle Charpentier. "Hang up your cloaks and tidy your hair, ready for lessons."

The two sisters meekly joined the ranks of enlightened scholars.

It turned colder overnight and by the next afternoon it was raining, with sleet streaking the rain. No one could go outside but the girls could not visit the rebels hidden upstairs because the headmistress decided that it would be a good opportunity for everyone to practise the recitations and songs for the prize day, which was fast approaching.

"It is only a pity that poor Madame Kieffer has such a bad cold," she said. "I told her to keep to her room, for her cough is dreadful to hear. We could do with a real music teacher in this school."

Madame Kieffer, Rémy's mother, had been a singer in her youth; on the strength of this she had been teaching music, but it was not a very satisfactory arrangement.

"Papa has found a man he thinks might do for a music master," said Seraphine. "We heard him playing the pianoforte when we were at home. His name is Henri Théry."

Claudine stared at her sister in horror, but Seraphine seemed unaware of the danger of drawing attention to their cousin.

Madame Bilsdorf was so interested to hear this that she sent a servant through the sleet to Hautefontaine with a letter, begging Monsieur de Trévires to send his protégé over on trial, to help with the prize day music, as Madame Kieffer was ill.

"A music *master* – that is quite the proper thing," said the headmistress with satisfaction, "provided he is married."

"Oh, he's married all right," said Seraphine. "But I think his wife is living somewhere else, with relations."

As they sat waiting for their turn to recite Claudine whispered, "How could you tell of Cousin – Citoyen Théry like that?"

"But he said that was what he was going to do," said Seraphine.

"You silly creature, it was only to be given as the reason for his being at Hautefontaine," Claudine said.

Seraphine gazed at her, blue eyes wide. "Really? Well, he need not come. Papa can find some excuse."

But he did come, the very next morning, brought by Monsieur de Trévires in the carriage. Rémy came too, to see his mother.

Thierry de Ravanger looked just like a music master, Claudine had to admit it. His snuff-coloured suit was neat but slightly worn and he bowed deferentially whenever Monsieur de Trévires spoke to him, though he always called him, emphatically, Citoyen, not Monsieur. Claudine thought it amused her cousin to play the part, and she became less anxious.

The girls were all very interested in the new master. They had a master for drawing but he was much older than Thierry, dry and grey-haired.

"Though this one is nothing much to look at," said Lucille Perrard, the beauty of the school, tossing her black locks. "And lame, too."

"But he has got a nice smile," said Annette Desroux sentimentally. She was recovering from a cold, her nose still red, her eyes watery. It seemed a pity, Claudine thought, that all the looks in that family belonged to the brother, Lieutenant Jules. She liked Annette better than Jules, but she was a dull girl – dull to look at and dull to talk to; one could only feel sorry for her, not be fond of her.

By the end of the afternoon's practice a number of girls had been won over by Citoyen Théry's smile and the musical ones were delighted at his skill on the pianoforte.

"Now we shall have some *real* lessons," said Lotte Poos, the earnest republican, jubilantly.

Seraphine was in fits of giggles. "He looks like a stuffed owl," she said, "and I do like his obsequious manner – you would never think he was a count."

Although they were alone, Claudine glanced nervously over her shoulder. "Do be quiet, Seraphine."

"Why should he be in danger? He has done nothing against the Republic – unlike your friend."

Claudine found it odd to have the rebel leader called her friend.

"The French suspect all aristocrats, especially *émigrés*," she said. "They hate them more than the peasant rebels."

But Seraphine, always an optimist, did not worry over her Cousin Thierry, and next day alarmed her sister by trying to make him laugh by her cheeky manner. However, she only succeeded in drawing on her head the wrath of Mademoiselle Charpentier.

"Citoyenne Seraphine! What a shocking way to behave! Apologise to Citoyen Théry at once and you are to write out two hundred lines this afternoon."

Thus it was that Seraphine was not with Claudine when she went out into the garden that day. It was now almost a week since she had seen the rebels and it was quite hard to believe they were still in the house.

Claudine found it difficult to slip away today; Annette Desroux hung on her arm, complaining of the cold as they walked in the paths of the parterre. It certainly was cold, for there had been a frost at night, a light snow had powdered the ground, and the wind was north east. But it was fine, the sun shone intermittently, pale but bright, and Claudine did not mind the cold. In the end, to shake of Annette, she said she was going to climb up to the ruins.

"I should go indoors, if I were you, Annette," she said. "This wind won't do your cold any good."

Since Annette did not want to climb the steep path to the old castle she took this advice, and Claudine quickly set off, alone, holding her cloak close, with her hands in a little fur muff.

She hoped to have time to go down by a path further along and so get into the house and find her way to the old Count's "hunting room".

"Though I daresay they won't let me in," she thought, suddenly remembering all those locked doors. How did they know when it was Lisel outside? She had forgotten to ask. Perhaps the best thing would be to find Lisel this afternoon and wait till another day for the visit, when Seraphine could go too. But then Claudine frowned, remembering her sister's behaviour about Thierry. It seemed to her irresponsible.

She climbed the path so fast she was quite out of breath when she reached the ruins and paused, in the shelter of a tumbledown wall, to recover herself. She looked across the valley, thinking how much more wintry it appeared than it had not two weeks ago, when she had first seen the rebel with the scarred face, standing below on the hillside. It was the snow, of course; although it was only a thin powder it whitened the ground, so that the bare trees showed up spidery and black. The river, down below, looked almost black too, by contrast.

"*Bonjour*, Concordia!" said a voice behind her which already she could recognise.

She turned, startled, to see Gabry standing by the wall, smiling.

He was wearing an old thick cape over his servant's clothes, with a red cap pulled down on his head, covering the bandage which she saw he still wore. But some of his black hair showed, curling over the edges.

"Oh!" she said. "It's you! What are you doing out here?"

Gabry laughed. "Do you think I ought to stay in bed for months, nurse?" he said. "Perhaps I would, if you came every day to do up my head – but you have deserted me. I haven't even heard you singing. Hard-hearted Sancta Cecilia! I listened, on your day, but – not a sound!"

The feast of Saint Cecilia, patron of music, had been that day on which Claudine had returned from Hautefontaine, as she now told him. She said nothing about Citoyen Théry; she had more sense of keeping a secret than Seraphine. She only said that practices for the prize day had kept her away since then.

"Besides, Lisel is looking after you much better than I could."

"Lisel is a good girl, but she is not as lovely as my *fantôme*," he said, taking a step towards her.

Claudine gazed at him, surprised by his proprietary tone. She could not help thinking it familiar in someone she scarcely knew, who, moreover, if not a peasant, was only an ex-soldier. Then she remembered the rumour of the Austrian agents.

"Are you an Austrian?" she asked abruptly.

It was Gabry's turn to look surprised; no doubt he could not see any connexion between his remark and her question. But he answered, "No, mademoiselle, I am a Luxembourger like yourself – though I expect Monsieur de Trévires would not consider my family as old as his!"

He smiled, and in spite of the twist the scar gave to his mouth, his smile made his hard face with its strong hooked nose much more attractive. He was looking down at Claudine just now with eyes full of kindness and amusement.

She said nothing and so after a moment he went on, "Lisel said you had gone home for your birthday. Now I wonder how many years you have been walking this earth?"

"Eighteen," said Claudine.

"Eighteen?" he repeated, evidently surprised. "I thought you must be younger, being still at school."

"I am only at school to encourage the others," said Claudine gravely, and could not imagine why he burst out laughing.

"My beautiful republican angel! It would indeed be an encouragement to have you in any school," he said, and suddenly took her hand.

Claudine quickly withdrew it and pushed it into her muff and she was taken aback when Gabry pursued it into that furry refuge. He put his hand inside too and closed it round hers, quite gently, but firmly enough to hold it. "I have caught you, little mouse," he said, and put his other hand round her shoulder.

Claudine had never been touched like this before; she was taken by surprise, not only by his action but by her own sensations. She stood there trembling, looking up at him with startled but not frightened eyes.

"What – what are you doing?" she said at last, hardly above a whisper.

"Losing my head," said Gabry. "I think, any minute now, I am going to kiss you."

Warned in this way, Claudine could have protested, pulled away, even have struck him with her free hand, but she did none of these things, because she found she felt no objection to his kissing her. Again she was surprised by her own reaction, surprised into silence, but it was not a hostile silence, and she did not resist as he drew her closer. Her hood dropped back and the wind blew her thick silky hair about, golden brown strands blowing across her face, and across his face too, now so close to hers.

He had taken his hand out of her muff and was smoothing the hair back; she felt his fingers caressing her cheek and in her hair. The muscles of the arm holding her felt hard, but the gestures were quite gentle.

"Claudine!"

It was the cry of a hoarse, breathless, youthful voice: Rémy's voice, shaken with shock.

Claudine, awakening from the sudden spell, turned her head over her shoulder and saw Rémy toiling up the last slope of the path.

Gabry too raised his head and looked over Claudine's.

Rémy stopped in his tracks, staring.

"Monsieur d'Erlen!" he said, with a gasp.

Claudine jumped back, freeing herself easily from Gabry's arm, and she too stood there staring at him. One of the Erlens of Villerange! And now those portraits in the gallery seemed to float before her, those dark eagle faces, the thick black hair, the greenish eyes – how could she have missed the resemblance?

Gabry was looking at the young man, annoyed, but wary.

"And who may you be?" he demanded.

Rémy had recovered some of his usual truculence. "Oh, you would not remember me, Monsieur le Comte," he said. "I was just the son of one of your servants – Rémy Lefèvre."

"I do remember you now, Citoyen Rémy," said Gabry, his face relaxing into a smile. "You were with my Cousin Thierry in England."

"Yes, and he sent me back to Monsieur de Trévires," said Rémy. "I am his secretary."

"So you propose to go and tell him I am not dead but have returned to haunt my own house?" said Gabry. "What an embarrassment for Citoyen Trévires! Don't do it, Citoyen Rémy, there's a good boy! I will take myself off to the woods and leave his young ladies in peace."

Claudine, still gazing at him, wondered how she could ever have thought he was a peasant, or even a soldier.

Rémy obviously hated this ironic way of talking.

"You would try to pass this off as a joke," he said. "But if you are truly Le Cicatrisé, you are an enemy of the Republic."

"You are perfectly correct, Citoyen Rémy," said Gabry coolly. "The Republic has no more determined enemy than myself. What are you going to do about it?"

Rémy glared at him but could think of nothing to say.

"Rémy, you won't give him away?" said Claudine anxiously. "He was wounded . . ."

Rémy turned to her then with an anguished expression in his blue eyes.

"Oh, Claudine, how did you meet him? How did you come to allow him to . . . Don't you know what a reputation he has with women?"

"I did not know who he was," said Claudine, blushing. "Even now, I don't know which of the Erlens he is."

"Gabriel d'Erlen, mademoiselle," said Gabry, with a bow, as if he had been in a drawing room and in court dress.

"The eldest – the Count of Villerange, in fact," said Rémy, adding scornfully, *"Ci-devant!"*

Gabriel smiled.

Claudine looked at him. "But you were really fighting with the peasants?" she said, doubtfully.

"Certainly, and I am not ashamed of it," he replied. "I came back to Luxembourg secretly, after the peace was made. We have misjudged the rebellion, for the Austrians are not ready. It was the conscription that made the peasants strike too soon. They could not stand being marched off to fight for the Republic, one and indivisible!"

He used the catch phrase of the Revolution with derision.

Rémy flushed. "I am surprised the peasants would follow you," he said. "Your family have a bad reputation as harsh and violent masters."

"Ah, but it is the French who have felt my harshness and violence," said Gabry, with his twisted smile.

Then his manner changed and he said abruptly, "Now speak up honestly, Rémy. If you think it is your duty to inform on me I will take to the woods forthwith. But if you are enough of a Luxembourger to give me a few days' grace, I admit I could do with a little more rest. The rebellion has failed. There is not much I can do now against your glorious Republic, except to try to get some of my men safely away. So! What do you say?"

Faced with this sudden choice, Rémy hesitated.

Claudine was thinking herself entirely forgotten, when Gabry turned to her and said, "Forgive me, mademoiselle, for talking business like this in your presence. I would much rather be talking to you!"

"Talking!" burst out Rémy resentfully. "You were embracing her! A young girl at school, Monsieur de Trévires' daughter! Nobody is safe from you!"

"Monsieur de Trévires has no business to have an angel for his daughter," said Gabriel d'Erlen, once more in his light ironic tone. "What has he done to deserve such a gift from heaven – in which he does not even believe? Angels should be bestowed on those who know how to value them." He smiled at Claudine, evidently not expecting her to be angry with him.

She was not angry, but she had become deeply suspicious, now that she knew him to be an aristocrat, a *ci-devant* land-owner, and with a bad reputation, Rémy said. And certainly, she thought, he had taken advantage of her.

"You let me think you were just a soldier," she said.

"You never asked me my name," he replied. "The others called me by it – Gabry is what I have always been called at home."

On the breeze came the metallic sound of the little hand-bell, ringing and ringing.

"Lesson time!" said Gabry amused. "Concordia, there are not many lessons you need – only one, which I should like to teach you myself."

"I've no doubt you would," said Rémy, glowering. He took Claudine's arm, and she allowed it.

But she said, "Don't give him away, Rémy. Think how dreadful it would be, not only for Papa, but for Cousin Thierry . . . Please, Rémy."

"No, all right, I will not," said Rémy ungraciously. "But he had better go away soon."

"Give me three days more," said Gabry.

"Very well," said Rémy and he hurried Claudine away down the path.

"After all, Rémy, he was shot in the head," she said, as they went. "He isn't fit to go into the woods yet."

Rémy gave an impatient growl. "Somehow men like that always get girls' sympathy," he grumbled. "Worthless brutes!"

CHAPTER
SIX

RÉMY was staying at the school because of his mother's illness, but she was not to ill to prevent his being invited that evening to supper with Madame Bilsdorf, the new music master, and some of the senior girls.

While Claudine was changing, Seraphine asked her what she had been doing in the ruins with Rémy. "I saw you coming down the path with him."

"I went up there by myself," said Claudine. "and that man – the rebel, was there. Rémy came later and saw him."

"And recognised him by his scar?" said Seraphine.

Her quickness defeated her own curiosity, for Claudine was glad to acquiesce, deciding that she need not tell her that Le Cicatrisé was also the Count of Villerange.

Seraphine was glad to hear that Rémy had promised not to report the rebel, but it surprised her. "It must be for your sake," she teased her sister. "Otherwise his devotion to the Republic would surely win!"

She was not going to Madame Bilsdorf's evening party, but sat on her bed in her school dress, ready to go down to supper in the dining room.

"I wish I was coming," she said. "I would tease Cousin Thierry!"

Later, in the headmistress's drawing room, Claudine thought it was Cousin Thierry who was doing all the teasing.

Madame Bilsdorf wanted the girls to sing a revolutionary song at the prize day. "I want Monsieur de Trévires to know that we are all devoted to the cause of the Republic," said Madame Bilsdorf ardently.

"But in order to convince him of our loyalty to the Republic, one and indivisable," said Thierry, dwelling on the phrase with pious solemnity, "do you think we should risk shocking his sense of propriety? I do not feel that Madame de Trévires would approve her daughters singing about bloody standards and such things."

"Good heavens, Citoyen Théry, are there such words in that song?" said the headmistress, taken aback. "That certainly would not do!"

"Let me sing you a verse of a composition of my own," said Thierry, modestly, going to the little clavier that stood in the room. And with portentous solemnity he sang to a hymn-like tune a piece of doggerel addressed to Liberty. Claudine suspected that he had invented it on the spur of the moment. She thought that Madame Bilsdorf must surely recognise his mockery, but she took the republican hymn quite seriously, and praised it with enthusiasm.

"Indeed, as it is concerned with the principles of republicanism and not with French patriotism," she said, "it is really more suitable to the occasion than the Marseillaise."

Claudine was glad Seraphine was not there; she could never have kept a straight face.

"Citoyenne Claudine, I must speak to you." It was Rémy at her elbow, and on the pretext of showing her a book he manoeuvred her away from the circle gathered admiringly round the clavier. They remained in full view but, if they spoke quietly, out of earshot.

"How did you come to meet him?" Rémy asked, in a low anxious voice.

No need to mention any name; Claudine knew well enough whom he meant. She described the first scene on the hillside but she did not say she had afterwards seen Gabry in the house. Rémy evidently imagined he must be hiding in one of the outbuildings and she did not choose to enlighten him.

"I suppose there is no longer much he can do against the Republic," Rémy admitted, reluctantly. "But it is just like him to start philandering with the first woman he meets, even if she is a young girl at school. You can't trust a man like that – he has always been the same. Ask Victoire, if you don't believe me."

Victoire was a Frenchwoman who had come to Villerange before the Revolution as a lady's maid; she was now in charge of the girls' clothes, with several sewing maids under her.

"She came here with his wife," said Rémy.

"Oh," said Claudine, gazing at him. "He is married, then?"

"Married? He was married at twenty," said Rémy. "To get more lands and riches – she was a French heiress. I last saw her when I was in England. They were on bad terms then; Monsieur d'Erlen always spoke of her unkindly. She was not beautiful and I suppose that after her château was looted he felt he had tied himself to her for nothing. Not that he let the marriage bond interfere much with his amusements. When I was here in '92 it was common talk that he was the father of a child by a French Marquise, a fugitive from the Revolution, who was here with her elderly husband. My mother said the baby looked a regular Erlen, green eyes and all."

Claudine felt some disgust at having almost succumbed to the charm of the shallow sensualist this man appeared to be. She did not speak.

"You won't see him again?" said Rémy anxiously.

Claudine shook her head. "Not if I can help it."

Then Madame Bilsdorf called her over to sing and she tried to put out of her memory those few moments with Gabry in the ruins.

All the same she sought out Victoire next morning in her sewing room. She was something of a favourite with the elderly Frenchwoman, who was not particularly republican in her outlook and thought most of the girls in the school low-born ill-mannered creatures. Madame de Trévires' daughters were different. Victoire always thought of them as Madame's daughters. She had no very high opinion of men and considered Monsieur de Trévires a blind fanatic.

"Victoire, you came here with the French Countess, didn't you?" Claudine said, sitting in her petticoats while Victoire mended a rent in her skirt. "What did you think of the family who lived here then?"

Victoire sniffed. "The men thought they were gods and could do as they pleased," she said. "My poor mistress – who agreed to the match with the eldest son to please her father – she had much to suffer here. But it is not proper to talk of it to a young girl like you."

"Well, but I have heard something about that Count Gabriel," said Claudine. "For instance, that he had an affair with a French Marquise, after his marriage. Is that true?"

Finding she knew that much, Victoire told her more. "Such an insult to Madame, to become the lover of a guest in the house," she said. "But in those days he was handsome – it was before he got that ugly scar – and he did just as he pleased."

"What scar?" asked Claudine, in order to learn more.

"Oh, in the face – it was done by a bullet in the battle when his father was killed, in France," said Victoire. "They were with the Prussians when they were defeated at Valmy by the revolutionary army. After that Madame went to England with her father and I could not attend her because I was ill when she had to leave. The young Counts were with the Austrians and retreated when they did, in '94, and we've seen no more of them. Good riddance, I say. I hope they were killed in the battles."

Reminded of the past, she talked on. "Men are so selfish," she said. "My poor young Madame never had good health. She had not the prettiness of that little Marquise, with her yellow hair. And Monsieur made no pretence of hiding his passion – everybody knew of it."

"What happened to the Marquise?" Claudine asked.

"Oh, her old husband took her to Trèves to have her child," said Victoire. "It was as like our young Count as two peas!" She suddenly cackled with laughter. "But he was served out, for she found another lover in Trèves, so I'm told. Not that a man like that will lament for long. He could always take up with some village girl, as his father did, or one of the servants as we heard had happened before we came, when he could not have been more than eighteen. Yes, that's why his pious mother wanted him to marry young, poor good lady. She thought it would cure his bad habits, but of course it did not, though she did not live to know that."

The handbell began ringing below and Claudine stood up.

"That bell!" said Victoire. "I can't see the use of all this learning – it will only give you bleary eyes. Most of the girls here would do better to learn deportment."

She finished her mending deliberately and so Claudine was late for the lesson. Madame Charpentier shook an admonitory finger.

"Dreaming again, Claudine! You don't want me to have to report you to your father, I'm sure."

Claudine sat down and opened her book. But she was thinking of Gabriel d'Erlen and trying to connect in her mind the arrogant young aristocrat of seven years ago with the rebel leader who had called her Concordia and would have kissed her if Rémy had not interrupted them.

After dinner she suddenly found Thierry beside her. "Citoyenne, your father wishes me to give you music lessons," he said.

But as they went out of the dining room together he said quietly, "I have heard that a certain cousin of mine is about and that you know where he is. Is that so?"

She looked at him, hesitating. "Yes."

"Will you show me, Claudine? I want to see him."

"I don't know if he will come out," she said. "But if we went to play on the harpsichord in the card room beyond the ballroom, we – would be quite near him."

"Excellent," said Thierry, seizing up some music and starting off through the gallery.

These unheated rooms had now become very chill and Thierry stopped. "Claudine, should you not take your cloak, if we are going out by the small side door, as I imagine we are?"

Claudine looked at him with her large pensive grey eyes.

"We don't have to go out," she said, after a moment.

"What, you mean Gabry is hiding in the house itself?" said Thierry. "What a nerve! But how like him!" He walked forward and then stopped again. "I know where he must be – in his father's love-nest, that he called his hunting room."

Claudine assented, but added, "They keep the doors locked and I don't know the signal. That's why I thought that if he heard the harpsichord he might come out to – to see if it was me."

Thierry gave her a searching look from under his heavy eyelids. I got the idea from Rémy that Gabriel had been playing his usual game with you," he said. "I don't want to run him down, but be careful you don't fall in love with him, Claudine."

Claudine was able to say with perfect truth that she scarcely knew Gabriel d'Erlen. But even as she said it she felt a little hypocritical. For although their meetings had been few they were hardly like a casual acquaintance.

They passed a portrait of Gabriel's father, only half visible in the dim shuttered light, but Claudine glanced involuntarily towards it.

"He's the one who will always be *the* Count of Villerange for me," said Thierry. "Formidable old fire-eater! Gabry has never really held the position because of the war. I wonder what sort of seigneur he would make? I don't think he has much head for business, but he'd be popular with the local men – the young ones, anyway."

"Would he? Why?" asked Claudine, as they went on through the shadowy ballroom.

"Oh, because as boys they all went about in a gang together," said Thierry. "I too, before I fell off the wall. We were the terror of the countryside! Gabry was always Captain and thought of the wildest expeditions. That's why I was surprised he had come back here, where he was so well known."

"He's only just come back," said Claudine. "He was fighting in another part of the country – or so he said."

She felt doubtful now if she could believe anything Gabry said.

They went into the end room, leaving the door open to admit light from the unshuttered passage windows.

"Now, play something he knows," said Thierry, retiring into a dark corner. "And sing too, please."

Feeling self-conscious, Claudine sat down and began the old ballad she had been singing in the ruins the day she discovered the echo.

She had not finished it when she heard the sound of a door clicking open and shut. Gabry moved quietly and the next moment he was standing in the doorway. When she stopped playing he said softly what she knew he was going to say: "*Attendez, fantôme!*"

Then he came towards her saying warmly, "I am very glad you have come, Claudine. I was afraid our friend Citoyen Rémy had frightened you away."

Claudine had risen; now she backed away from him, uncertain what to say, because she knew her cousin Thierry was watching and Gabry did not.

He immediately followed her across the floor. "Don't run away, *ange de la liberté!*" he said. "If you were not afraid to come back here, surely you are not going to refuse to speak to me? No, that would be too phantom-like!"

"Mind your step, Gabry!" came Thierry's cheerful voice from the corner. "There's another *revenant* watching you!" He stepped out of the shadow, limping forward quickly, his hand held out.

Gabriel swung round. "Thierry! Wonderful!" he said, joyfully, grasping his hand and then gripping him by both arms. "But what on earth are you doing here?"

Thierry explained that he had come to find his uncle, Abbé de Lamerle, and Willibrord's son, and Gabry immediately said, "Young Josy is with me – with my men in the woods. I can send him a message by Lisel's brother, Wenzel. As to your Uncle Xavier, we must have him out of prison at once. Where is he?"

"We don't know yet," said Thierry. "Gautier de Trévires is going to find out."

Gabriel grinned. "First time I've found myself working with Citoyen Trévires!" he said.

"You seem to have worked fast with his daughter," said Thierry, smiling, but with a slight edge of disapproval in his voice.

"Concordia!" said Gabry, turning back to Claudine. "Forgive me for so rudely forgetting your presence. But I have not seen Thierry since his marriage. Remarkable!" he added teasingly, "but it doesn't seem to have altered you a bit, Cousin!"

Claudine was trying to fit his two characters together, reminding herself that here was someone not to be trusted, who had scorned his wife and blatantly pursued another woman in this very house. But in his presence she found it difficult to maintain her indignation. He seemed too warm-hearted to be as callous as his past actions suggested.

Gabriel sat down on the stool with his back to the harpsichord and began talking eagerly to his cousin. He asked after someone called Ludovic.

"He is very well," said Thierry. "But why didn't you write, Gabry? It would mean so much to him."

"I wrote from Vienna," said Gabriel. "But since the peace I've been here. One can't write to England from somewhere that is called part of France now, my dear Thierry, especially if one is trying to disrupt government services rather than using them!"

"You've been here as long as that?" said Thierry. "Nobody knew where you were – not even your brother Dominique."

"I don't inform Dominique of my intentions," said Gabriel dryly. "Besides, he's been in Italy, getting defeated by this Corsican, General Bonaparte. Now look here, *mon cousin*, you have become too much like an Englishman, living in that little island. Do you think it would be safe to write letters all round saying, 'I'm just off to start a rebellion in Luxembourg – I'll keep in touch'?"

Thierry laughed. "I might have guessed where you would be," he said. "But were you in charge of this rebellion, Gabry?"

"No." said Gabriel, his expression and his voice changing. "It was not properly organised and everything happened too soon. It's been a tragedy, the whole thing. I can't tell you . . . so many poor fellows have died in vain." And after a moment of sombre silence he went on, "I came down here to rescue a couple of my own – we did it too, I'm glad to say. It was afterwards that I got my bullet – and that has not been serious, thanks to the angels – my guardian one and this little republican angel, who can't bear to speak to me now that she knows I am a wicked aristocrat instead of a mistaken but honest peasant."

He smiled at Claudine, who said gravely, "It's not because you are an aristocrat."

Thierry laughed. "No, Gabry, it's your personal rather than your political wickedness which has upset my little cousin. So you must stop behaving to her like a romantic outlaw and be rational."

Claudine expected Gabry to be annoyed at this but he only laughed and said, "I promise you, mademoiselle, I will be good."

She could not feel much confidence in this assurance, considering the way he was looking at her, but all the same she found it difficult to maintain a cool detachment. Gabriel d'Erlen was by far the most interesting and attractive person she had ever met, and it was not the least part of his attraction that he so evidently found her fascinating. All the time he was talking to his cousin his eyes kept coming back to her, as she sat quietly listening.

But presently Thierry took out his watch. He had a much better sense of time than Claudine. "It will soon be lesson time," he said, "and I have to give one to Citoyenne Poos, who has a very heavy hand on the pianoforte."

Gabriel rose from the stool. "Well, if you want to get into father's Bluebeard chamber," he said, "give one loud knock and two quick ones, three times over. The same to you, mademoiselle."

"You're hopeful, inviting her into Bluebeard's chamber!" Thierry teased him.

"But I am not Bluebeard," said Gabry, laughing. "Nor was father, to do him justice. He was quite popular with his women – much kinder to them than he was to us, the old devil." As they walked to the door he added, "Besides, I have Norbert with me – remember Norbert Wagener? He is the perfect chaperon, I assure you, as good as any Mother Superior."

They parted with laughter, but Gabriel managed to kiss Claudine's hand and went off looking, as Thierry remarked, pleased with himself.

"I am fond of the wretch," he said, "but I don't trust him an inch when there's a pretty girl about."

"I wonder you like him so well," said Claudine, "when it was he who pushed you off that wall and made you lame."

"Pushed me? He didn't push me," said Thierry. "He did play a trick on me, pretending to be stuck in a high place in the ruins, so that I had to go along a wall to get to him, and it collapsed."

"I'm sure I was told he pushed you," said Claudine.

"Well, that is just what happens to stories about Gabry," said Thierry. "They get worse as they go round."

"What about the Marquise?" asked Claudine at once.

Thierry glanced at her. "So you've heard that? No – that was true, I'm afraid. Gabriel certainly has another son besides Ludovic, though he does not go by his name."

"Oh – is Ludovic his son?" Claudine said. "Why did he ask you about him?"

"Because he's living in my house," said Thierry. "We're very fond of him. He's got the Erlen look, but not the temper, fortunately."

They were passing through the gallery and Thierry waved his hand at one of the pictures. "I don't know if you can see that – it's of Gabriel and Dominique at about the age we were when the unfortunate wall episode happened. It was being painted while I was here, lying on the sofa watching."

Peering at the picture in the dim light Claudine remembered having seen it before and speculating about the two handsome boys in outdoor dress, with their dogs, and the elder with his gun, against a romanticised landscape, with the ruins of the old castle in the distance.

"It was started before my accident," said Thierry. "Gabry was feeling sensitive about the ruins afterwards and wanted them painted out, but the artist was too fond of his handiwork."

Claudine stared at the fifteen-year-old Gabry, with his clear-cut features and curling black hair, obviously so confident, so pleased with his dog and his gun, and no doubt with his own appearance; and she smiled.

Thierry noticed the smile. "What amuses you, *ma cousine*?"

"Only that he looks as if he owned the whole world," she said, "even then."

CHAPTER
SEVEN

MADAME BILSDORF suddenly decided to hold the prize day concert in the ballroom and on the second day after Rémy had recognised Gabriel d'Erlen that part of the great house swarmed with servants folding back shutters, lighting fires in the marble fireplaces, dusting gilded picture frames and arranging chairs in rows.

There was no possibility of going to look for the rebels – not that Claudine wished to do so, at least she thought not. She felt extremely suspicious of Gabry's intentions towards her and not at all sure of her own powers of resistance – and that made her feel ashamed of herself.

She was so very absent-minded that day that she was sent to bed early as a punishment. It was no punishment to Claudine, who liked lying warm in bed, listening to the wind whistling outside, and for once not listening to Seraphine's chatter.

The wind was certainly whistling and even though the windows were shut the curtains moved in the draught. There was a soft patting noise going on and suddenly Claudine whispered aloud, "I believe it's snowing!"

She jumped out of bed and ran barefoot across the boards to look out. Snow was whirling out of the darkness against the glass, white splurges melting on the pane.

Suddenly she thought of the rebel peasants, Gabry's men, as he had called them, hiding in the woods. Where did they hide, in weather like this? And she wondered where he would be hiding, when he left the château. Had he perhaps gone already, alarmed by the servants so busy on the floor below him?

Claudine's feet felt cold and she ran back to her bed, snuggling into the warm shape of herself still there under the bedclothes. But she still went on thinking about Gabry till she fell asleep and when she woke it was with the conscious-

ness that this was the third day. "Give me three days," he had
said to Rémy.

"Oh, what a lot of snow to fall in one night!" cried
Seraphine, dancing about to keep warm as she tried to put on
her clothes without standing still.

Snow lay white all over the ground, over the paths and
flower beds and terraces, over the hillside. The ruins and the
bare trees stood out dark against the whiteness.

"Won't it make it easier for the French to track down the
rebels in the snow?" said Claudine uneasily, as she brushed
her hair.

"Claudine, you've changed sides about the rebels!" her
sister teased her. "What would Papa say?"

"I'm not on any side," said Claudine, "I just don't want
our Luxembourgers killed, that's all."

In her head she heard Gabry's voice saying: "No,
mademoiselle, I am a Luxembourger like yourself." That was
before she had known he was a Count. Claudine sighed. She
had liked him better as an ordinary rebel, she thought. But
perhaps that was because knowing who he was meant knowing he had a wife somewhere, and that he had had a mistress
and other women too. Rebel or Count, however, his
behaviour to her had been the same; he had even started by
kissing his hand to her, she remembered. He must have been
watching her for minutes before she had seen him down there
on the hillside with his companions; he must have been
listening to her singing and calling to the echo.

"Claudine, wake up! You haven't got your stockings on.
You'll be late for breakfast," said Seraphine.

That afternoon Thierry held a full rehearsal in the ballroom. It was not exactly warm in there, even though two
large fires were burning in the marble fireplaces.

"Sing well, Citoyennes, and you will warm yourselves
up," said Thierry.

He seemed perfectly at home playing music master to a
school of girls.

While some of the performers were executing their solos,
by voice or instrument, the members of the choir were
allowed to walk about at the other end of the room. Younger
members were actually sliding in the gallery, unknown to
their elders.

Claudine went to the windows which gave on to the courtyard inside the castle and there she saw some men in woollen caps and scarves, sweeping the snow off the paths. As she looked, Claudine saw one figure, much taller than the others, which she could not mistake, even though he was more muffled up than the oldest man at work out there.

"It's to hide that scar," she thought.

Gabry was at the end of the line and nearest the windows and she saw him glancing towards him. The next moment he saw her and smiled. He came towards the window, sweeping vigorously.

Claudine was alarmed. What was he doing, showing himself like this? Why hadn't he gone away? The afternoon light was already fading; inside the house a few candles had been lighted and the rehearsal would soon have to end, since the school could not afford to illuminate the great ballroom.

Gabry came close to the window and because the ground outside was lower his face was below hers, below the sill. He looked up and made a signal with his hand, motioning her to go along the passage past the card rooms. As well as the door to the garden below the old Count's private stairs, there was another on the opposite side, into the courtyard, used by the kitchen staff. Gabry wanted her to meet him up there. It was quite clear to Claudine and his look was urgent, pleading.

She glanced back into the ballroom. Nobody was watching her. Most of the girls were standing round the fires. Seraphine was sliding in the gallery with the younger girls. Claudine thought she could slip away.

She left the window quietly and walked into the passage. As she was going along it she heard Thierry calling out, "Choir! Citoyennes, assemble for the final chorus!"

"Oh dear," muttered Claudine. But having come so far she decided to go on. She began to run, as lightly as she could, fast over the wooden boards, so fast that as she turned the corner at the end she ran straight into Gabry, who was standing just round it, waiting for her.

Running into Gabry was like running into a tree; he seemed as hard as that to Claudine, and the gasp she gave at the impact was more of pain than fright.

Trees, however, do not immediately catch hold of a person who runs into them. Gabry caught her readily and held her close.

"My dear angel, are you hurt?" he said, with a hint of amusement in his concern.

"Yes!" said Claudine resentfully. And then, realising that he was making no movement to release her but instead was plainly enjoying the chance which had thrown her into his arms, she said, "Let me go!"

"No!" said Gabry, imitating her tone of voice. But he was smiling.

"What do you want?" Claudine demanded.

After all, she had come because he had signalled a need to see her; he must have something he wanted to say. And as he was just looking at her she said it again, impatiently, "I can't stay. What do you want?"

"You," said Gabriel, softly but with decision.

Claudine was suddenly swept with anger: it raged through her like a fire. She had never been so angry in her life. His arm was under her right arm. She doubled her fist and punched him as hard as she could in the crook of the elbow. He gave a startled, smothered yelp and she broke away from him.

He looked so surprised at her attack that Claudine laughed. But then she found tears starting to her eyes and she ran away, crying.

"Claudine!" he called after her, as loud as he dared. "Come back! Claudine!"

But she ran on, stifling her tears, brushing them savagely away with her sleeve, ran into the ballroom and crept to the back of the choir. She could not have sung a note, but none of the girls noticed.

Thierry, however, facing the choir, saw her there. After the chorus was concluded he dismissed the girls with a word of praise but stopped Claudine. When they were alone he said to her gently, "Now what is it, my child? You came in crying. Was it Gabriel?"

Claudine felt she was going to cry again; she nodded.

"Confound him," said Theirry. "Wait here – I will go and speak to him."

He went limping away and Claudine sat down near the fire, staring into it.

Presently Thierry came back. "I can't find him," he said. "And they have left Bluebeard's chamber. There was no answer to the signal." He leaned over Claudine, concerned for her. "It is too bad of Gabry," he said. "He must know you are not like the women he has pursued before." And then he added, in some puzzlement, "But it is not like him to go after a young girl, an unmarried young lady. No, he never was that kind of seducer. Unless this wild life he has been living for the last year has changed him – I suppose it might."

Claudine got up. "Well, he's gone now," she said. "Don't worry, cousin, I am not going to be silly about it, I promise you."

Thierry looked relieved, but he walked with her as far as the front stairs, which she went up to go to her room and wash her face.

"Citoyen Théry's favourite," said Lotte Poos, jealously, to Annette Desroux.

The next day everyone was up in good time and dressed in their best by eleven in the morning. The concert had to be held early, before light faded. The parents and friends, as they arrived, were given refreshments in the school dining hall, which had once been the principal dining room of the Counts of Villerange. the girls in their white dresses and best sashes, their hair brushed and gleaming, walked about, handing round plates of cakes.

Monsieur and Madame de Trévires were the guests of honour in this enlightened establishment, but the chief excitement for most of the girls was the expected arrival of Lieutenant Desroux and his friend Gaston Ferrand, who had just been made a Captain. They would be in uniform and attended by soldiers, for it was hardly safe for French officers to ride about the country alone. They had not yet come, for it was some distance from Luxembourg. Even when people began moving to take their places in the ballroom, now become a concert hall, they had not yet arrived, to the disappointment of Annette, who had been saving many special delicacies for her brother. But Madame Bilsdorf had invited the officers to dinner afterwards; only a very select party stayed to dinner.

Lisel was helping with the refreshments, pouring wine into glasses that stood on trays. Claudine saw her looking anxiously in her direction and presently went up and asked her if there was anything the matter.

"Oh, mademoiselle, I want your help," Lisel whispered. "That Norbert left something of his master's behind and he asked me to bring it to him at the side door before the concert began, and I can't get away. Would you take it for me? You are the only one I could ask to do it."

"Of course I will," said Claudine. "Which door? The one they used?"

"No," said Lisel, "the one you young ladies use, at this end of the gallery. If you open the door and look out, I expect he will come."

She put her hand in her pocket and then pushed something into Claudine's hand. It felt like a ring; glancing covertly at it Claudine saw it was a heavy gold signet ring with a dark red stone. She looked up, surprised, but Lisel whispered, "He doesn't always wear it, of course. Norbert was supposed to keep it safe. He was very worried to have left it behind."

Claudine went away, the ring clutched in her left hand. She walked from the dining room across the entrance hall and through the anteroom of the gallery. The double doors which led to the gallery were folded back, and people were strolling through, on their way to the ballroom. On the right was a door to the lobby where the girls kept cloaks and clogs, Claudine went through the door, shutting it behind her, shutting out the subdued chatter of people passing, and most of what warmth there was in that wing of the house. The lobby struck chill, with a paved stone floor, the cloaks hanging round the walls on wooden pegs and the cold winter light coming only dimly from a high narrow window.

Claudine went across to the door into the garden, drew back the bolt and unlatched it, looking out. It seemed very bright outside; the sun was shining on the snowy ground.

There was a man standing at the corner of the house, wearing a leather cap with ear flaps, a high collar turned up, and a neckcloth almost round his chin. It was not Norbert. It was Gabriel d'Erlen.

He came quickly to the door and Claudine was so surprised that she stepped back into the lobby without saying anything. Gabriel followed her in, closing the door behind him.

"Claudine, I had to see you," he began.

"But Lisel said . . . oh, was Lisel pretending?" said Claudine, bewildered.

"She did it to help me," Gabriel said. "I could not go without seeing you again, Claudine. I wanted to say how sorry I am that I caused you distress yesterday."

Claudine stood back against the cloaks by the wall, watching him with suspicion. She said nothing, only looked at him with her wide cloudy grey eyes.

"I meant only to ask you to tell Thierry where we were going," he said. "But when you ran into me, I lost my head. It was too like a dream come true when someone so lovely runs into one's arms. Can't you understand that, Claudine?"

Claudine felt she understood it very well; she found this quiet, self-controlled Gabriel even harder to resist than the laughing, teasing one.

"Well, I am glad if you are sorry," she said doubtfully.

"I am sorry I annoyed you," said Gabry. "I am not at all sorry for loving you."

Claudine stared up at him, wishing the light was better. He had pulled off his cap, but he was standing with the window behind him, his face in shadow.

"Are you teasing me?" she demanded. "You can't love a person you hardly know."

"I can," said Gabriel with decision. "I almost fell in love the first time I saw you, and heard you calling to the echo. I quite did, the second time, when you bravely walked in to help a groaning rebel. You see, it is a long standing attachment, mademoiselle."

Claudine could not help smiling. "You know how silly you're being?" she said. "I don't believe a word of it."

"Just as well," said Gabriel, but he sounded dispirited. "I am really not in a position to declare my love, but I thought it better than to let you think it a mere amusement that could be practised with anyone."

Claudine was surprised. He spoke quite seriously; could he really mean what he was saying? She could think of no reply and so she made none.

Gabriel interpreted her silence as hostility. "You can't bear the sight of me," he said gloomily. "All right! Don't worry – I am going away now. Tell Thierry, to the Roman Temple."

"Where's that? I've never heard of it," said Claudine.

"He knows," said Gabriel. "His father had it built, more or less – mine never knew or cared anything about antiquities."

"I'll tell him," said Claudine. "And," she hesitated, "and please don't think I hate the sight of you. I wish you well, monsieur."

"Oh, you blessed creature!" he said. "How kind your little heart is!" He was smiling again now. "Perhaps, since I am going away, you would allow me just so much of my dream as to kiss your hand?"

She held out her hand and he took it but then for a moment he just stood there, holding it. Claudine became aware that he did not want to leave her; she felt a restlessness in him, an unhappiness that touched her more than his former self-confident laughter.

"As you are going away," she said breathlessly, "I think you might kiss me, if you want to very much."

"Dear angel, I do," he said, putting his other hand on her shoulder, "but I don't think it is wise. It is much better for you to forget all about me and somehow I don't feel that kissing would help that. It's more like a beginning than an end, my love."

"Yes, I see," said Claudine, in a small voice. Her heart was beating hard; but she felt a sort of disappointment within her.

"Perhaps I will see you again, when we are free," he said. "But for now, it is farewell. So, *adieu, très chère*."

He leant his cheek against hers and stroked her hair but did not kiss her.

But they were so absorbed in one another that they were taken by surprise when the door from the garden suddenly opened.

Rémy was saying, "*Bonne chance!* It's unlocked, as I hoped."

Then he saw them and stopped abruptly on the threshold. Behind him were two young French officers and, it seemed to Claudine, a whole company of soldiers.

"Ah, I see we've interrupted a little love scene!" said Jules Desroux, grinning. "But can it be one of the young ladies with one of the stablemen?" Then his tone changed, with the shock of recognition. "Why, it is Citoyenne Claudine!"

"And that's not a stableman," burst out Rémy in a rage, "that's the *ci-devant* Count of Villerange, whom you ought to know, for you've been chasing him round the country for weeks, with the peasant rebels."

As it happened, the unscarred side of Gabry's face was towards the door, and in that dim place he might have escaped recognition but for Rémy's disclosure.

"You thought he'd been shot dead, but he wasn't," said Rémy, in his fury that the hated aristocrat was still here, still pursuing the innocent Claudine. "The Erlens have nine lives, like cats – they've always been known as the devil's familiars. There! Look at his face! Don't you recognise him now?"

"Le Cicatrisé!" shouted Gaston Ferrand.

"Oh, Rémy!" cried Claudine, in an agony.

Gabriel wasted no time in speech. He leapt straight for the door into the anteroom, and Claudine, hardly knowing what she was doing, ran after him, just in front of the French soldiers. She heard Ferrand giving quick orders, directing men to go outside the house and watch the exists.

"And don't kill him – I want a capture," he said.

She remembered what he had said at Hautefontaine about making an example at the guillotine and felt sick with fear.

Gabry turned left in the anteroom, making for the front of the house, but just as he was within a yard or two of the doors the headmistress appeared, escorting Monsieur and Madame de Trévires, and a few other favoured guests, to take their places for the concert.

Faced with what seemed to her like one of the outdoor servants gone mad, and a tall wild-looking man at that, Madame Bilsdorf let out a shriek of alarm.

Gabriel doubled back and ran through the doors opposite, into the gallery. There were still a few people strolling through it on their way to the ballroom, staring at the portraits of the Erlens; most of the families who sent girls to this modern school had never been inside the château before.

Because of the gaping people Gabry's flight up the gallery was not as rapid as it might have been; he had to dodge round them, and in so doing he slipped on the polished boards and nearly fell.

It was not enough to allow Gaston Ferrand to catch up, but it delayed him, and as he ran to the ballroom the French were close behind and shouting, "Stop him! Stop that man!"

They had pushed past Claudine, but she was still hurrying along after them; she hardly heard her mother calling from the other end of the gallery.

"Claudine! What are you doing? Claudine, come here at once!"

She could only think of Gabry; they must not catch him.

The chattering throng already in their seats for the concert were all jumping up in consternation, but were much too startled to obey Ferrand's command to stop the man who was running through the room.

As Gabriel ran into the passage alongside the card rooms, three French soldiers appeared at the other end, with cutlasses and bayonets in their hands. They must have run along the outside of the house and entered by the door at the foot of the old Count's private stairs. If he went on, Gabry would be caught between the two parties in that narrow passage.

He swung round and cut back into the ballroom before Ferrand's men had caught up with him, running across the end, which was empty of chairs, for neither the school nor the audience was large, towards the tall windows.

Claudine was only half way up the room, the French soldiers near enough to the last row of chairs to be able to push violently through them and make for their quarry as he ran and jumped for the window seat at the end.

The sills were three or four feet above the seats; when the ballroom was built nobody had thought of looking out of windows – the company within had been the attraction.

Gabriel leapt up on the seat but tall as he was, he could not reach the catch in the middle of the window. Before he had time to get up on the sill the nearest couple of soldiers came at him, one with a cutlass and the other with a bayonet. He turned and kicked the cutlass down, dodged the bayonet, which stuck in the wooden panelled embrasure, and scrambled up on the sill.

Claudine reached the last row of chairs and stood clinging to the back of one, staring desperately at this struggle in the window. The other soldiers had come up now; Gabriel surely had no chance.

But as soon as his foot was on the sill he had wrenched the catch sideways and pushed up the bottom sash. The window was heavy and still. He only got it up about a foot before one of the men, jumping on the seat, caught his ankle.

Gabriel kicked backwards into the man's face and he lost his footing and fell off, knocking one of his fellows aside. Dropping down on the sill and pushing one leg out of the window, Gabry got his shoulder under the sash and heaved.

All this had taken no more than a few moments of time; the

guests were still in confusion, but all on their feet and turned round, watching the chase. Claudine saw Thierry limping up the side of the room near the windows. As he had been on the dais at the other end, he had the whole length of the room to go before he could reach the scene of action. But what could he do, in any case?

Then, before he had got any further than the other end of the row of chairs where Claudine was clinging, trembling and staring, another soldier with a bayonet made a lunge. Gabriel was astride the sill, crouched down, trying to get through the narrow space; it was his left leg which was still inside and with his left arm and shoulder he was still heaving at the lower sash to get more room.

Crouched under the window like this, it was impossible for him to do more than give sideways kicks at his assailants with his left foot, as he tried to squeeze through the gap. The man with the bayonet evaded him and, as he got his foot on the seat, aimed his weapon higher. He succeeded in driving the point through Gabry's upper arm, pinioning it to the wood of the window frame.

"Well done, Creuzet!" shouted Gaston Ferrand. "You've skewered our chicken all right!"

For the first instant Claudine had thought it was only Gabry's sleeve which was pinned to the window, but then she saw by the jerk of his body and the way he pressed his head against the frame that the keen blade had pierced the flesh. It made her feel sick and giddy.

The soldiers swarmed round the window and Gabriel was caught from all sides before they thought it safe to pull out the bayonet. They dragged him, still struggling, down to the floor and one of them shut the window again. It was as stiff to close as it had been to open.

Suddenly, after all the shouting and struggling, there was a lull. The French had caught their man. Now they pulled him to his feet again, holding him by the arms, and one pushed a pistol against his back.

Gaston Ferrand was triumphant. He was also curious, interested to discover that the rebel leader was one of the hated *ci-devant* aristocrats. He stood in front of Gabry, scrutinising him closely.

"So! We've got you, slippery eel that you are," he said. "Caught you skulking in your own home, eh? Seems you couldn't keep away from the young ladies!" And he laughed, a coarse guffaw.

Claudine felt hot, though more with anger than shame. Yet it was an anguish to think that this vulgar sneer was almost true, in so far as it was because he wanted to see her again that Gabriel was in the house today.

Suddenly she caught sight of Rémy, watching. He was red in the face and silent; she could not tell whether he was ashamed, or exulting in what he had done.

The soldiers still held Gabriel as if they expected him to make another bid for freedom at any moment. But Claudine thought it hardly possible; he was breathing hard still from the stress of the chase, and the bayonet wound was bleeding through the sleeve of his torn coat.

But he stood upright all the same, taller than his guards, taller than Ferrand, and looking more like a Count d'Erlen than Claudine had ever seen him. He looked down at Ferrand with an expression of disdain. He said nothing at all.

Gaston Ferrand did not like it. He was a revolutionary who had risen by his ruthless fanaticism and devotion to the cause.

"So you think the representative of the Republic is not worth speaking to, you arrogant devil!" he said angrily. "Well! You will have to answer to the tribunal when you are tried for your crimes against the people."

Gabriel d'Erlen answered him then, but he spoke in the Luxembourger German. Everyone in that room understood him, except the French conquerors.

"I have committed no crime against *our* people," he said. "I have been fighting with them against you Frenchmen because we don't recognise your right to rule us. Luxembourg is not part of France and it never will be."

Ferrand could make a good guess at these patriotic sentiments.

"Speak French," he said, irritated. "And don't pretend you aristocrats aren't brought up to speak it from your cradles – such is the superior civilisation of France. Sensible men count it a privilege to belong to our nation in this new era of liberty."

"So! You can't even understand our speech," said Gabriel in French. "And yet you expect us to be grateful for being conquered. What fools you fanatics are!"

"Be silent!" shouted Ferrand, enraged

"Citoyen, it was you who commanded me to speak," said Gabriel, with sarcasm.

This altercation produced some smothered titters among the girls, many of whom, being Luxembourgers, felt more sympathy for the rebel than the officer – his being an aristocrat, however wicked, only made him for them a more romantic figure, especially as he looked, at the moment, exactly like everyone's idea of a robber count.

Aware that his prisoner was stealing his thunder, Ferrand said angrily, "Don't pretend to be a patriot! I know your sort – you are in the pay of the Austrians. You make use of the poor peasants here, send them to their deaths, to give the Austrian Emperor an excuse to start war against France again – to put the aristocrats back into power. That's all your fine talk amounts to, my noble patriot! You're nothing but a mercenary, out for your own ends. Well! We shall soon see you marched out to the guillotine in Luxembourg and that will be the end of your boasting and sneering."

While this tirade was in progress Madame de Trévires had come bustling up the side of the big room. Now she addressed the Frenchman in matter of fact tones.

"Citoyen Capitaine, you have no doubt done your duty in arresting Monsieur d'Erlen, but you must realise that this is causing our estimable Madame Bilsdorf a great deal of inconvenience. Now, you cannot start for Luxembourg with Monsieur d'Erlen in that state, bleeding from a bayonet wound. So I suggest we call on the services of our excellent barber surgeon from Mersch, who happens to be present, since his talented daughter is taking part in the school concert. Let him dress Monsieur d'Erlen's wound, and do you and Lieutenant Desroux attend our festive occasion as it was planned before this unfortunate incident."

The barber surgeon, recognising the accents of authority, had come forward as soon as she had mentioned him.

"I shall be happy to be of service to Madame," he said, bowing.

Gaston Ferrand found himself firmly organised by this brisk little lady, the wife of that well-known republican, Citoyen Trévires. Gabriel d'Erlen was escorted along the passage and round the corner towards the kitchen quarters, and all that Captain Ferrand could do was to issue strict orders to make sure his prisoner did not escape.

Claudine had kept on staring at Gabriel as long as he was in view, but when she saw the last of the back of his black head, she suddenly came to herself, aware of the crowded room, and realising that she would soon have to face the questions of her parents. She saw her father coming towards her now.

And then she felt something hard clutched in her left hand and, with a shock, remembered taking it from Lisel – it seemed an age ago.

It was Gabriel d'Erlen's ring.

CHAPTER
EIGHT

CLAUDINE suddenly knew that she did not want her parents to see Gabriel's ring. She pretended she had not noticed her father coming and walked away from him towards the fire, as if to warm herself. Then, straightening her dress with nervous fingers, she contrived to drop the ring down the front of her bodice. It stuck between her breasts, but the dress was so modestly made, with a frill round the not very low neck, that, glancing down, she saw it was not visible. But it was strange to feel Gabry's ring just there; it vividly brought back the feeling of his hand caressing her. Her skin was not the sort to blush easily and the slight colour as she turned to meet her father might have been caused by the heat of the fire.

"Claudine!" he said, coming up to her. "My dear child, what were you doing, running after Monsieur d'Erlen in that extraordinary way?"

"Oh Papa! It gave me such a fright," said Claudine. She was breathless from nervous fear of giving something away, but it gave the impression of simple agitation. "I went into the lobby and he came in . . . to hide, I suppose. But then Rémy let the French officers in by that door. The Captain was giving orders to catch him when he fled . . . Monsieur d'Erlen, I mean . . . I just ran to see what happened."

Gautier de Trévires had grey eyes, very like Claudine's, except that they were not set in dark lashes like hers. Eyebrows, eyelashes and hair were all a light sandy colour, which gave him a faded look. He peered at his daughter, face to face, for they were much of a height, and only saw an innocent frightened child.

"Poor darling," he said, affectionately, taking her arm. "Come, you are not fit to sing in the concert. Come and sit by me and listen."

Everyone was now settling down again, though there was a buzz of talk about the recent excitement. Claudine did not at all want to sit in the front with her father, stared at by all, and she persuaded him to let her take her place at the back of the choir.

Claudine had never admired her cousin Thierry more, for no one could have guessed how nearly he was concerned with the fate of the rebel leader just captured. He looked pale and serious, but tapped his music stand to get their attention with his usual mild authority.

"Citoyennes, courage!" he said softly. "Show how well you can sing!"

The concert went fairly well, considering everything. Gaston Ferrand and Madame de Trévires came back into the room together after it had begun. Claudine thought her mother looked remarkably composed; but then she had dealt with wounded men during the war, and most efficiently, too. She sat down beside her husband and applauded vigorously at the end of each performance. What was more, she had evidently succeeded in persuading Ferrand to stay to dinner, no doubt wishing to give Monsieur d'Erlen as much time as possible to recover before he was taken off to Luxembourg.

All the same, taken he would be, and Claudine felt so sick at the thought of it that she did not go into the dining room but slipped into an alcove off the entrance hall, asking Seraphine to tell her mother she was going to her room. Seraphine was plainly longing to hear all that had happened, but she would have to wait. She hurried away and Claudine leant back against the wall, feeling too tired to move.

It was some time later that she saw Thierry crossing the hall towards the gallery wing, carrying two large bottles of wine and two tankards – and he was finding it difficult to manage them all at once.

Claudine jumped up and ran after him. "Where are you going? Let me carry your mugs."

Thierry handed her the tankards as they went into the anteroom. The doors to the gallery stood open. There was no one there now.

"I didn't want Gabry's guards to miss their entertainment," he said, with a wry smile. "I made sure the officers had some of the old Count's best vintage and I've sent potent stuff to the kitchen for the soldiers. But I thought I'd better make sure of the guards myself."

"What do you mean?"

They were walking up the gallery now, Thierry with his bottles under each arm, past the portraits of the dead counts.

"How old Monsieur de Villerange would have cursed at these fellows getting his best wine!" he said, glancing up at the belligerent Comte Bertrand as he passed him. "But it's all in a good cause." And as she still looked inquiringly at him, he said. "We can't let them get as far as Luxembourg, Claudine. We could never get Gabry out of their clutches once they had him in the fortress. If they are full of wine, something might be done on the way."

"Oh – a rescue?" whispered Claudine. She had not thought of that.

"Well, I've sent Lisel to her brother," said Thierry. "They will have to manage that part of it. It was your mother's delaying action which gave me the idea, though I think she was only worried that poor Gabry was going to lose half his blood before they ever got him to the guillotine."

They walked up the empty ballroom together. Remembering that stabbing blow through the arm, Claudine shuddered.

"Is it a bad wound?" she asked, anxiously.

"It could have been worse," said Thierry. "Your mother says no artery was cut and it should mend well. I have not seen him – I was conducting you girls, and wondering if one of them was going to faint. But you must be as tough as your mother, Claudine."

As they passed the card rooms he said, "Sometime I'd like to know how they found him out."

"Rémy told them," said Claudine, her indignation against Rémy suddenly returning in full force.

Thierry stopped dead. "Rémy? Gave Gabry away to the French?" he said.

Claudine remembered how much Thierry had done for young Rémy Lefèvre. "Perhaps it was the surprise of finding him here," she said hastily, for she did not want to tell Thierry that Rémy had been furiously jealous at discovering her, as he had thought, once more caught in the embrace of an aristocrat he hated.

Because Claudine looked so innocent, and indeed till now been innocent of any deceit, everyone always believed her.

Muttering something about speaking to Rémy, Thierry marched on, but he talked no more. It had plainly been a shock to him to learn that Rémy had betrayed Gabriel to the French.

They turned the corner where only yesterday Claudine had run into Gabry; and how she wished now that she had not reacted with anger – for if she had not run away from him crying he would not have taken the risk of coming to look for her today. "It's all my fault," Claudine thought in anguish.

Thierry soon stopped at the door of a pantry and knocked loudly on it. One of the soldiers opened it; he looked a typical revolutionary, with long lank hair and angry eyes.

"Citoyen," said Thierry with a bow, "the compliments of Citoyen Trévires and he sends you these bottles of wine from the *ci-devant* Count's cellars."

"Very kind of him," said the soldier, opening the door wider. His companion, a more bonhomous type, seized on the bottles with noisy exultation.

Through the door Claudine could see Gabry, sitting on the floor and leaning against the wall, with his arm in a sling and his legs stretched out. Then she saw that his ankles were tied together with cord, one each side of the table leg; his shoes were removed. Evidently the men, though armed, were taking no chances.

Gabry had looked round at the sound of Thierry's voice but he gave no sign of recognition either of him, or of Claudine. She was somehow disappointed. In the ballroom, too, he had never once looked at her, she now remembered.

Thierry took the mugs from her and handed them to the soldiers.

"Only two?" said the more talkative man. "What about him?"

"We can't waste good wine on a bad aristocrat, can we?" said Thierry, looking at his cousin from under his heavy eyelids.

"I call that mean, considering it is my wine," said Gabry, with vigour. "Was that an order from Citoyen Trévires, the stingy fellow?"

"No, it's my own idea," said Thierry. "Why should a stinking *ci-devant* have the chance to fuddle his wits before he goes to meet his fate? I want you to know exactly what's happening to you, my fine patriot, and not miss a thing, even on the journey to Luxembourg."

"Vindictive, isn't he?" observed the cheerful soldier, who was busily opening a bottle.

"Home-grown republicans are the worst sort of traitor," said Gabry, staring at his cousin with contempt.

Thierry ignored him, gave a farewell greeting to the guards, remarked that he did not suppose they would leave for an hour or so, and drew Claudine away.

She glanced over her shoulder and saw Gabry looking at her, but still he did not even smile.

As they retraced their steps Claudine asked, "Were you hinting to Gabry that there might be a rescue?"

"Of course, and he understood me," said Thierry, with a smile. "Now, if they do give him a drink, he will be careful not to take too much, so as to be on the alert."

"He sounded as if he despised you," said Claudine. "And why did he look at me as if he had never seen me before?"

"My dear child, how could he do anything else?" said Thierry. "Especially after that fellow Ferrand's coarse insinuations that he was here after one of the young ladies! I know he upset you yesterday by behaving as if that was indeed his object. All the more reason not to show that you were known to him. His morals may not be very reliable, but his manners at least are those of a gentleman."

Claudine felt ashamed. She said nothing.

Thierry said kindly, "All this has been a great deal too much for you, my poor little *cousine*. Now I am going to take you up to old Victoire, and she will bring you something to eat and drink, and pet you a bit. That's what you need."

Claudine's eyes were ringed with shadow as she looked at him. "But Victoire . . . won't she know you?"

"Yes, she does know me, but luckily we have always been friends," said Thierry. "She hasn't much use for Gabry, because she took her mistress's side in that unfortunate marriage. But she just allows me to pass as human."

Claudine very soon found that old Victoire's feelings for Monsieur de Ravanger were warmer than that. Sitting by the fire, with a quilt over her shoulders, eating bread and milk like a child, and comforted by being treated as one, Claudine heard that Monsieur de Ravanger had always been thoughtful, good-hearted, a kind master, unlike the masters of Villerange.

Victoire had not seen the capture of Gabriel d'Erlen. She was surprised to hear that he had been in the country over a year, but not surprised to hear that he had taken part in the peasant uprisings of the autumn.

"Always ready to fight," she said. "A regular band of brigands he made of the village lads when he was a boy, so I've heard tell."

"I never hear much of his brother," said Claudine.

"Because Count Dominique was the quiet one," said Victoire. "They never did get on. Quite unlike each other in every way, except in features. You could tell they were both Erlens, with those curving noses and curling lips, black hair, green eyes and the rest of it – ugh! I don't care for any of them." The old woman hunched up her shoulders and pursed her lips. "Now, drink up your coffee. I put some brandy in it, as Monsieur de Ravanger suggested I should."

Victoire's room was in the back wing of the château, overlooking the stables and outhouses, built in a second quadrangle round a cobbled yard. The winter afternoon was already beginning to close in when Claudine heard the jingle of harness, horses' hooves stamping, and men's voices. She jumped up and went to the window. The French were leaving.

Claudine looked down into the yard, looking for Gabry. She soon saw him, for the white sling showed up in the grey twilight, though his coat, with the torn sleeve flapping loose, was buttoned across at the top. He was bareheaded and she could still see where she had cut off his hair round the scalp wound; it could hardly be properly healed yet, she thought, and now he had been wounded again.

One of the soldiers was putting a rope round his waist and tying his right hand to it, behind his back. Having done this, they had to help him on to his horse, a docile-looking nag. One mounted soldier managed it by a leading rein; another took the end of the rope from his waist. It would certainly be difficult for Gabry to escape on the journey.

As she watched, Claudine's heart sank. Even if Gabry's men had got the message from Thierry, how could they achieve a rescue? There seemed to be a lot of soldiers, as the party formed up, with the prisoner in the middle. But certainly they did seem a bit the worse for drink, shouting, laughing and not very steady in their movements.

The two officers presently came round the corner from the house drawing on their gloves. Jules Desroux was, as usual, swaggering, but Claudine thought it could easily turn into a stagger. Both of them stopped, laughing, near Gabry and Ferrand said something in a jeering tone which Claudine guessed to be insulting, from the silent stare with which it was received.

Gabriel looked as he had when first captured, sitting very straight-backed, with his chin up, and looking down that formidable nose with an expression of proud disdain.

Old Victoire, who had come up behind Claudine, remarked, "Just look at him! He could be sitting for a caricature of his order."

His order, his estate of nobility: this was how the old Frenchwoman thought of it.

"If they send him to the guillotine, that's how he'll look on the way to it," said Victoire.

"It's brave at least, Victoire," said Claudine, gazing down at that stiff silent figure, so unlike the Gabry who had laughed and teased her, and wanted to kiss her.

"Brave! Of course – that's all the old Count cared about," said Victoire, scornfully. "His sons must never show fear. It didn't matter to him what else they did. That one has been brought up from his cradle never to admit he's beaten. But now it looks as if he is. Well, although I never did like him, I don't approve it. Cutting off king's heads, noble heads – that's not the right way to do things. Once you begin, it seems, you can't stop. Men! They can't feel they exist unless they're killing someone else."

Claudine's trembling sigh cut short the old woman's mutterings. "There! I'm upsetting you! Come away now, and put it out of your mind."

"No," said Claudine. "I want to watch him go."

And she did watch, till all the party had ridden out through the stable gates, formed up anew, and gone trotting away towards Luxembourg.

When she could no longer see Gabry's back she turned from the window with a sigh. Afterwards, she curled up on Victoire's little old sofa and fell fast asleep.

She thus missed her mother, who failed to find her and had to leave for Hautefontaine, assured by her husband that poor little Claudine had only accidentally been involved in Monsieur d'Erlen's spectacular attempt to evade capture.

Later, Claudine went down to supper with the girls, to be greeted with cries of, "Wherever were you?" from Seraphine.

Directly after that light meal they were sent up to bed. The single candle stood on a little round table by the bedstead. Seraphine unlaced her sister's bodice and out fell the ring, which Claudine had quite forgotten. It had slipped down to her waistband long before and now it rolled on the floor.

Seraphine made a dive and a grab, and got it first.

"Give it to me!" cried Claudine, trying to catch her sister's wrist.

"Let me look at it first," Seraphine said. She ran to the candle and examined the ring. "It's a signet . . . why, here's a little dragon. Isn't that the Erlen crest? Claudine!" she looked up, wide-eyed. "It's Monsieur d'Erlen's ring!"

So then at last Claudine had to tell her everything – or almost everything – that had happened.

Seraphine was fascinated by the tale. "But now I've seen him I can't think how you didn't guess who he was," she said. "He looks exactly like the portraits in the gallery. I tell you the one he's most like – the Thirty Years' War Count, only without a wig, of course."

Claudine thought that Seraphine would probably have recognised Gabriel d'Erlen at once. "How slow I am," she said. "He must have thought me a fool."

"Not a bit – for he's in love with you," said Seraphine.

"Don't be silly," said Claudine, who had carefully left out of her story every encounter which could be construed in this way.

"I'm sure he is," said her sister obstinately. "Otherwise why did he send the ring, so that he could see you today? But Claudine, it is just like you never to tell me how handsome your brigand was! In spite of that scar he looked splendid, standing there in the ballroom, and making that odious Ferrand look such an ass."

But Claudine could not bear to discuss Gabry's looks when she feared that the next she heard of him would be that he had been brought before the revolutionary tribunal. She pretended to be more tired than she was and refused to talk longer. But in the dark she lay turning Gabriel's ring in her hand, thinking of him. At last she pushed it on to her middle finger and closed her hand over it.

CHAPTER
NINE

IN the morning Claudine put Gabriel's ring on the thin chain with a religious medal on it, which she wore round her neck, under her dress. Her mother had given it to her at her first communion, just before the war began. Medal and ring chinked together till she settled them inside her bodice, but they were invisible.

As the two sisters went downstairs in the dim winter morning they heard sobbing and saw Annette Desroux come out of Madame Bilsdorf's room. The headmistress was with her, and her arm was round the girl. Claudine had never seen her doing that before; she was not a demonstrative woman, always stiff, even giving the impression of having been stuffed, a lay figure in correct clothes.

Annette's face was red and swollen and she stumbled along, crying and choking. The Trévires girls stood on the flight above, looking down. Then they saw Mademoiselle Charpentier come out of the same room and ran down towards her.

"What is wrong with Annette?" Seraphine asked her.

"Oh my dear girls, what a tragedy! Poor Annette, her brother – that handsome lieutenant who was here yesterday – he's been shot down by those peasant rebels. They attacked the party taking that wicked man, the *ci-devant* Count, to Luxembourg, and poor Lieutenant Desroux was shot in the lung and is likely to die. Your father brought him back here, as it was nearer."

"Papa?" said Claudine in surprise. "Is he here?"

"Yes – it was after you had gone to bed and he insisted that no one was to be wakened. That's why poor Annette has only just heard the news." Mademoiselle Charpentier seemed, in a way, to relish the tragic situation.

It was Seraphine who asked, "What about the Count? Did they rescue him?"

"I believe so," said Mademoiselle Charpentier. "At any

rate the rest of the party went on to Luxembourg. Your father only brought the lieutenant and his servant here."

"And mother, I suppose," said Seraphine.

"Oh yes, all the Hautefontaine people – young Lefèvre as well."

The girls did not meet their parents till after breakfast, when they were summoned upstairs to the best spare room, where their mother was sitting up in bed drinking coffee and their father, fully dressed except that he was wearing a loose dressing gown instead of his coat, was standing by the window with his cup in his hand.

"My dear girls, we are taking you home with us," he said, as they came in and curtsied. "There has been altogether too much excitement here lately. It will do you no harm to have a longer holiday than usual."

"Good! Good!" cried Seraphine, skipping about as if she were six rather than sixteen.

Claudine sat down on the end of the bed. "Maman, we have just heard about Annette's brother. Is he going to die?"

"Who can tell?" said Madame de Trévires. "I suppose, being young, he may pull through, but . . ." She made a gesture with her small plump hand.

"Do tell us about it," said Seraphine. "Did you come in for the fight?"

"Fortunately not," said her father dryly. "No, when we arrived on the scene there was no sign of a rebel – even Monsieur d'Erlen had vanished."

"Of course, he was their object," said Madame de Trévires. "That man Ferrand was furious at having lost him; he was cursing everyone, though it was his own fault for letting them drink too much. Poor young Desroux had taken too much too, I'm afraid. It seems he was going to shoot Monsieur d'Erlen when one of the attackers shot him. They all jumped up out of nowhere in the twilight, the French say."

"I can't think how they knew of Erlen's capture, let alone that they would find him on the road there," said Monsieur de Trévires.

Claudine wondered what he would say if he knew that Thierry de Ravanger had been responsible for this, and for seeing that the French soldiers were half incapacitated by drink.

"Well, I cannot be sorry Monsieur d'Erlen has escaped,"

said Madame de Trévires. "He is a brave patriot, whatever you say, Gautier."

"It depends what one thinks best for one's country," said Monsieur de Trévires coolly. "Now, fetch your things, girls."

The sisters went along the passage towards their room and on the way they met Rémy Lefèvre, coming to visit his employer for orders.

Claudine had told Seraphine that Rémy had given away the Comte de Villerange to the French; she was still indignant and it had been some relief to accuse him to her sister.

And it was Seraphine who said now, "Rémy! I'm never going to speak to you again! How could you do such a dreadful thing as to betray Monsieur d'Erlen to his enemies?"

Rémy was looking at Claudine as he replied defensively, "Well, haven't you heard? He's got away this time."

"Of course we've heard, but that doesn't excuse you," said Seraphine. "If he had been executed, it would have been your fault."

"He said he'd be gone in three days and he wasn't," grumbled Rémy. "He didn't take me seriously enough to care what I did. Besides, all he was doing here was to run after Mademoiselle Claudine."

Claudine turned her face away, but did not say anything.

Seraphine said, "Well, it's no business of yours, Rémy."

"No," said Rémy, savagely. "Only that I knew him. The first time, before she had guessed who he was, I warned her and she said she wouldn't see him again. But she did! You did, Claudine – you let that man kiss you, knowing what I'd told you about him."

"What did he tell you about Monsieur d'Erlen, Claudine?" said Seraphine, realising that she had not had the whole story out of her sister after all. "Kiss you! Did he really?"

"Oh, be quiet, both of you! Don't fuss over me!" cried Claudine. "Rémy, once and for all, I can make up my own mind what I am going to do about Monsieur d'Erlen or anyone else. But you were wrong. He was not kissing me. He came to apologise. He was saying goodbye."

Rémy's laugh was not amused. "I've never seen a more loving farewell then," he said, in a sneering tone.

Claudine felt both angry and miserable; it was hateful to have that private moment with Gabry talked about and argued over by other people.

"Oh, leave me alone!" she said, with almost a sob, and ran away, past Rémy and on up the next flight of stairs to her room.

When Seraphine followed her there shortly afterwards, with unaccustomed tact she said no more about Gabriel d'Erlen.

And so they left Villerange and went home to Hautefontaine, standing now in beechwoods all bare, at the beginning of December. A few days later they heard that Jules Desroux had died.

For a week or two, life suddenly returned to normal for Claudine. They were at home, they went about their accustomed tasks and pleasures; it was winter and more snow fell.

Then the term ended at the school and Thierry de Ravanger came back to Hautefontaine, but not for long. Seeing Willibrord, through the open door, packing in his room, the girls stood looking in and Seraphine said, "Oh, Willibrord! Is Cous – Citoyen Théry going away?"

"Yes, mademoiselle, but if all goes well, you may see him again before he leaves the country."

"If all goes well?" Claudine repeated. "What do you mean?"

Seraphine added, "There's no one to hear, Willibrord. Do tell us."

"But I am not allowed to talk of it, so there's an end of it," said the stocky little man, pursing his lips. "There's no stopping him once he's made up his mind, no matter what the risk."

"Is it to do with Uncle Xavier?" asked Seraphine at once.

"You're a great deal too quick, mademoiselle," said Willibrord.

And so, although he would say no more, they knew that Thierry was going to do something for Xavier de Lamerle.

Thierry seemed in good spirits that evening and made them laugh by appearing with his hair powdered. "Don't I look a real grand seigneur, now?" he said.

"No, you look a real old man!" said Seraphine, laughing.

Thierry glanced at his aunt, who smiled, but her eyes were anxious. "You look very like Xavier," she said.

The girls did not realise that this was Thierry's object till about a week later, when their mother came bustling into their bedroom.

"Well, it has worked – I never thought it would," she said, plumping down in a chair by the fire. And in answer to their eager questions she told them that Thierry had succeeded in getting her brother out of the castle where he was imprisoned.

"It's a very old dodge indeed," she said. "Thierry dressed himself in black, as a notary, wearing a double set of clothes. He got two sets of false papers, applied to visit Xavier, went one day and told him the plan, and on his next coming, carried it out. Xavier went out as the notary and after the guard was changed Thierry came out as the notary. Willibrord says he does not think Xavier's absence was noticed for some time, as he had a cell to himself."

"Oh, how clever of Thierry!" cried Seraphine. "So that's why he put powder on his hair! And borrowed those spectacles from Papa – what a fright he looked in them."

"He said he felt cross-eyed afterwards," said Madame de Trévires, laughing. "Xavier wore his own spectacles, of course. I wonder the guards did not recognise him but in prison he has been wearing a long soutane again, and his bands, and a skull cap he had with him. I suppose in stockings and a hat he looked sufficiently different, and Willibrord says he made a convincing imitation of Thierry's limping walk. Besides, as he was not considered an important prisoner he was not well known to the guards. Anyway, it worked. I never thought it would."

"Can we see Uncle Xavier tomorrow?" Claudine asked. She had always been fond of this quiet scholarly uncle.

"They are not here – Thierry would not risk compromising your father," said Madame de Trévires. "After all, it was Gautier who found out where Xavier was held and he tried to secure his release by legal means, though he failed in that. No, they are hiding somewhere in the woods near Villerange – some kind of special place, where he thought we might visit them before they set off for England, which won't be till after Christmas. Thierry is worried about Xavier's health, whether he can stand the journey."

"I wonder if it's the Roman Temple, where they are?" said Claudine.

"How did you know?" her mother asked, in surprise.

Claudine, remembering that it was from Gabry that she had heard of this hiding place, hastily murmured something about its being mentioned by Thierry, when they were at Villerange.

"Didn't his father build it?" she hazarded, recalling what Gabry had said.

"Yes, old Monsieur d'Isenbourg was a great man for antiquities," said Madame de Trévires, evidently satisfied by this explanation. "Some peasants found this Roman pavement in the woods, the other side of that little river behind the ruins at Villerange. It's hidden in a dip in the trees. I don't know whether it really was a temple in Roman times but Monsieur de Ravanger was convinced of it, and so he persuaded the Comte de Villerange to build a little Roman Temple there as a summerhouse, though it was too far from the château to be much used. I remember a picnic there when I was a girl, when it was just finished. Oh, what performance it was, getting all the food and wine carried there! Clémence, Thierry's mother, was delighted with it and said she should like to live there. How the old Count laughed! She would be cold there in winter, he said."

"But maman, it's winter now," said Claudine. "Won't they be cold?"

"I daresay they will make charcoal fires which won't smoke," said her mother. "Now, for goodness' sake say nothing about it, not even to your father. He must not know of it – though I daresay he has guessed it all. But for his own sake we must keep it secret."

Claudine found she was wondering more if she would see Monsieur d'Erlen again than thinking of her uncle, and this made her ashamed. It had been a great relief to hear that Gabry had escaped, but now that it was some weeks since she had seen him, the terrifying excitement of his capture had worn off, and it was their other meetings which came more frequently to her mind. She could not, in fact, put them out of her memory. She was always thinking of him, wondering about him. Everyone thought her more dreamy and forgetful than ever.

Sometimes she would take out his ring, when she was

alone, and look at it. A great thick thing it seemed, far too
large for her slender fingers. There was the Erlen dragon
carved on the red stone and the motto under it, so small that
she could not decipher it: it was in Latin.

Seraphine had suggested it must be: "*Non serviam*" – I will
not serve. "The devil's motto!" she had said, giggling.

But Claudine could not feel that Gabry was typical of the
wicked and proud Erlen family; she could not believe him to
be more than, perhaps, conscienceless about women. But
wasn't that enough? She did not want to see him again. But
she was thinking all the time of the Roman Temple, and if he
would be there, when they went.

CHAPTER
TEN

IT was now within a few days of Christmas, and as this feast could not be celebrated in Monsieur de Trévires' republican household, his wife decided that it would be an excellent day on which to visit her brother.

"But we will go to Mass here first," she said, "for Xavier may not be able to say it."

They drove early to the village for Mass, ate breakfast with Monsieur de Trévires and set off across country to Villerange. It was a cold grey day but not snowing, and the roads were clear.

They did not approach the château but took a road which led them over a narrow bridge crossing the river into which Gabry had fallen when he was shot by the French soldiers. Beyond it was extensive woodland and the road was a private one belonging to the Erlen estate, narrow and little used. But it did go through to join a public road, near another village, and Madame de Trévires had planned to say she was visiting there and had taken a short cut, if she was stopped. But she was not stopped. She was very well known in the district and most people now thought of her husband as the owner of Villerange, because he had set up the school there.

Presently they had to leave the carriage and walk up a track towards the Roman Temple, which could not be seen from a distance because it was in a hollow. They were startled when a man jumped out of the thickets into the road before them; he was wearing rough clothes and holding an ancient musket.

"Oh, it is you, Madame!" he said in the dialect, and grinned. "We are expecting you, but we have to keep a watch."

"We?" said Madame de Trévires. "Who is 'we', may I ask?"

"Us deserters, as the French call us – runaway conscripts," said the young man. "There's a lot of us here today because the father is saying Mass for us."

They went on and presently reached the edge of the little combe where the Roman pavement had been found. A classic temple of stone with four pillars and a pediment stood there, with a wide semi-circular paving in front of it. This was not the actual Roman floor but an enlarged copy which had been made to old Monsieur de Ravanger's orders. Just now it was filled with men, all kneeling. On the steps of the temple an altar had been rigged up and there stood the priest with his back to them and his hands raised in the ancient attitude of prayer, saying Mass in whispered Latin.

Madame de Trévires and her daughters joined the back of the assembly, standing on the slope above the pavement, looking down. It seemed strange to Claudine to attend Mass in this open solitary place, with so many young peasants who had rebelled against the victorious republic. She saw Thierry at once; he was serving the mass for his uncle, handing him the wine and water. It was minutes later that she saw Gabriel.

He was kneeling near the front of the crowd on the pavement, with Norbert next to him and just behind there was a small square young man with red cheeks, whom she felt sure must be Willibrord's son Josy. Gabry's black head stuck up above all the others near him. She could only see the back of his head, but recognised it instantly.

At the consecration the visitors knelt down too, on the hard winter earth of the hillside, but afterwards Madame de Trévires made them stand up.

Presently the priest turned round to give communion and Claudine heard her mother draw in her breath. Xavier de Lamerle looked much older and more gaunt than when they had last seen him; he was only in his fifties, but he looked an old man. But as the peasant soldiers came forward and knelt to receive communion, he moved tranquilly along the line, putting the slivers of wafer, the bread of life, into mouth after mouth.

Gabry received communion. She thought all the men there did. Some went to relieve the guards on watch and they came down in their turn.

At the end of Mass they suddenly all began to sing an old carol of Christmas. Seraphine glanced at Claudine, with tears in her bright eyes. It was moving to hear those young men, caught in the trap of war, singing the old song of peace on earth.

Afterwards, when the assembly broke up, Madame de Trévires made her way across the paved floor towards the Temple, into which her brother had gone as if it were a sacristy. His rebel congregation had found him vestments and Thierry was now helping him off with them. His sister stopped at the steps and then suddenly saw Gabriel.

"Monsieur d'Erlen!" she said. "I did not know you were here. But I'm glad you got away all right."

He had seen them already, as Claudine had been aware, but had made no move to address them till her mother spoke. But now he came forward and bowed to her, with as polite a greeting as if he had been welcoming her to his château.

"And are these your daughters, Madame?," he said. "I think I once saw them, as very small girls, at Isenbourg. Now they look almost too grown-up to be the daughters of such a youthful mother."

Claudine gazed at him, hoping she did not look as surprised as she felt. She remembered what Thierry had said about Gabry's reason for not seeming to recognise her but it made her feel odd to be treated by him as a stranger.

Madame de Trévires was laughing at his compliment, but pleased all the same.

"Claudine was greatly upset by your capture at Villerange, Monsieur d'Erlen," she said. "You may not recall it, but she was the girl in the lobby when you ran through it."

"Madame, I had to run very fast on that occasion," said Gabry, smiling. "So I am all the more happy to meet Mademoiselle Claudine now, in peace."

"It was very rash of you to come to your own house, monsieur," said Madame de Trévires. "You are too easily recognisable."

Gabriel put his hand up to his scar and laughed. "This, you mean? Well, I shall be leaving Luxembourg soon."

"I am glad to hear that," said Madame de Trévires. "For this Gaston Ferrand has sworn to hold you guilty of the death of poor Lieutenant Desroux and won't rest till he sees you pay for it."

Gabriel frowned. "How does he make that out? I could not shoot anyone with my hand tied behind my back. In fact, he would have shot me, if one of my men had not got him first. I am sorry if he was a friend of yours. He was not a Luxembourger, surely?"

"No, French, from Lorraine," said Madame de Trévires. "Believe me, I don't hold you accountable, monsieur. Desroux was a soldier and it was a risk of his profession. But they gave him a military funeral in Luxembourg and this Ferrand, who is a fanatic for the revolution, has made a great song about how he is going to bring you to justice for your crimes against the people. So I hope you will leave the country as soon as possible."

"I shall go with Thierry and Monsieur de Lamerle," said Gabriel.

Madame de Trévires looked up at him in silence for a moment and then said, "I think you should not wait for them. They are not wanted by the French to the same degree as yourself."

Gabriel smiled. "I think I can dodge Ferrand all right," he said. "But here is Monsieur de Lamerle."

The Abbé came out and embraced his sister and then his nieces, and they all went into the Temple, which behind its façade boasted a little room with seats, a table, and windows high up in the walls. There were rolled-up mattresses in the corner.

"Thierry and I sleep here," said Xavier de Lamerle. "We are amazingly comfortable. These good young fellows look after us so well. One brings milk from his father's farm. Of course, all the people are on their side and help them."

He turned away to cough. He was emaciated and looked extremely ill.

"My dear Xavier, you are not well," said his sister sadly.

"No, I suppose not," he answered. "But I feel much better now that I have got out of that damp fort."

He began to tell them about the escape, with many chuckles, which ended in coughing.

Presently Willibrord and his son came in and began to set the table. Thierry said, "Where's Monsieur d'Erlen? Lay a place for him, Willi."

He went outside and presently returned with Gabriel, who sat down with them to this unusual Christmas dinner.

Claudine still felt it strange to be in company with him like this. She had never till now met him in an ordinary situation. This meant that somehow they had already become quite intimate without any social acquaintance. Sometimes she felt he was a different person, sometimes that they were both playing a game. But one thing was the same: he was just as quick to talk to her and tease her as before and somehow he managed to sit down next to her at the table.

"Mademoiselle Claudine, have some of this wine – it is from Villerange," he said. "Thierry thought it a pity to waste it all on those dolts of republicans, so he got Willibrord to bring some along. This time I can have some too!"

He was smiling sideways at her, so that she knew he was reminding her of the time she had come to the pantry with Thierry, when he had seemed not to know her.

Seraphine, who was sitting opposite, remarked, "It is funny to be at table with you, Monsieur d'Erlen. Somehow I can only see you running away from French soldiers!"

Gabriel laughed. "I don't know what my father would say at an Erlen's gaining such a reputation!" he said. "However, no doubt I shall soon be running towards them for a change, as I intend to join the Archduke Charles."

"Straight away?" said Claudine. It was borne in on her that he really was going away and would be leaving one form of danger only for another. She turned her eyes to him, those large eyes with irises like a grey moth's wing, and there was a silent crack in her quiet voice, as anxiety strained it. "Must you rejoin the Austrian army straight away?"

Gabriel said, with a slight twist of his mouth, "It is much safer fighting in an army, you know. Once scarcely ever has to run away alone. Everyone runs together and sometimes one can even save one's baggage."

Claudine had to laugh, though she could not believe in the safety of army life. She found, almost to her surprise, that Gabry was an interesting and amusing person to be with, even in ordinary circumstances. Not that the present circumstances were particularly ordinary, but her mother's presence made it seem more like a winter picnic than a meeting in the rebels' hiding-place.

After dinner the younger members of the party went out to see the Roman floor behind the Temple, and Thierry, pointing out the figure of a centaur, remarked: "He must be the ancestor of your family, Gabry!"

Then, as it was a fine afternoon, they went walking up through the wood towards a place where Gabry said, they would have a view of the ruins of the old castle of Villerange. The occasion became more like a picnic than ever.

Both Thierry and Gabriel were wearing farmer's clothes, with short boots and leggings, and Gabry had an old leather coat; but neither of them looked much like a farmer. Thierry's face was too intellectual, Gabriel's too aristocratic for the part, Claudine thought. Few of the local peasants moved with Gabry's quickness and energy; in spite of his height he had the balance and control of a man trained to the pitch of physical discipline – something Claudine had not fully realised before, since when she had first met him he had been suffering from the effects both of his head-wound and the violent fall down the hillside. Now he seemed to have recovered completely, and though he still carried his left hand in his pocket, to remind him not to use that left arm too much, it hardly impaired his vitality.

They all stood for a while on the little knoll, looking across the narrow valley, up the steep slope to the broken walls and arches of the ruined castle, standing against the pale misty grey sky of the year's end.

"My dear Gabry, I can't think how you did not break your neck, tumbling down there," said Thierry.

"Your erstwhile protégé, Citoyen Rémy, would no doubt ascribe it to the well-known alliance between my family and the devil," said Gabriel, with his twisted smile.

"I am very disappointed in Rémy," said Thierry sadly. "In spite of his republican opinions, I would never have thought him capable of betraying one of us to the French."

"But I understand Citoyen Rémy very well," said Gabry. "I know why he did it – I might have done the same to him, had our positions been reversed."

He had Claudine's arm in his, and she felt him press it.

But when Thierry asked him to explain, he would not. "No – but believe me, he thought he had reason to hate me," he said.

Thierry remarked, "Well! I cannot see you treating your worst enemy like that, whatever you may say."

"Maybe not, because it's more in my power to beat my enemies myself," said Gabry.

Thierry was evidently surprised that he should make excuses for Rémy, but dropped the subject. He set off down the wooded path with Seraphine; Gabriel and Claudine followed, after stopping once more to look back.

"I can still see you up there, *fantôme*," said Gabriel. "Singing to your echo . . . like a vision, you were." Then he turned away. "But it is better still to have you here, so close." And he put his arm round her.

Claudine stopped walking. "I thought I was to forget all about you, Monsieur d'Erlen," she said.

"Monsieur d'Erlen!" he exclaimed. "After starting with Gabry, you are not allowed to go back to such a formal address."

"But what would maman say if I were to call you Gabry?"

"Ah, maman!" he said. "Tell me, do you think she disapproves of me as much as your father does?"

"She usually thinks the opposite to father," said Claudine, which made him laugh. "Why do you ask?"

"Because the moment I saw you today I realised that I am not cut out to be an altruist," said Gabriel. "I don't want you to forget me a bit. In fact, I refuse to part with you."

"What do you mean?" said Claudine thinking he sounded remarkably gay. "You said you were going to join the army again."

"But one doesn't spend one's life in the front line," said Gabriel. "I asked about your mother's view of me because I believe she may be more open to persuasion than your esteemed papa."

And as she still gazed up at him, puzzled, drawing her fine brows together, he went on, "It's usual to ask permission from a young lady's parents before proposing marriage to her."

"Oh!" cried Claudine and her eyes blazed as they had in the passage at Villerange. "Oh, how could you mock me so! I hate you!"

She broke away from him but stood there, so astonished that she did not run away, as she had before.

"Mock you?" said Gabriel, startled. "My dearest angel – why should you accuse me of such a horrible crime?"

"How can you talk of marriage," Claudine said, "when we know you are married already?"

He was surprised into silence, but after a moment said quietly, "Claudine, didn't you know my wife Anne-Louise is dead? She died in England, more than a year ago."

Claudine gasped out, "I didn't know."

"I thought you would have heard that from Thierry," he said. "That's why he's looking after my son. I didn't want

Ludovic brought up by his French grandfather, whose mind stopped working when the Bastille fell."

Claudine tried to collect her scattered wits. "He may have told my parents," she said, "but I didn't know."

There was suddenly a silence between them. It was so quiet in the winter woods that Claudine could hear the sound of the little river flowing, far below. She could hear nothing else, no voices; Thierry and Seraphine must be far ahead.

Then Gabriel said, "Claudine, I know I have not behaved at all properly towards you, and I certainly don't deserve that you should consent to be my wife. Nevertheless, that is what I want – more than anything in the world."

And as she said nothing, but only stood looking at him uncertainly, he presently went on, "Once I'm across the Rhine I can make some appearance of respectability – I've got money there. If you would only risk it and come with me, I could look after you very well, I promise you."

Claudine meant to answer calmly, but, once she started to speak, her emotions carried her away, like a stream in flood.

"But you know it's all nonsense, don't you?" she said. "You don't really mean it, you can't. It's just because you saw me up there singing – I'm something new for you, a little country girl who doesn't know anything about the world. You've got to go away and you want to take your new toy and so you ask me to marry you. Heavens! What would you do with me, in a place like Vienna? You would be bored in a few weeks. And whatever your other wife felt about it, I would not put up with your mistresses! I should go away and leave you to them. But no, I won't begin something I know will only end in misery."

Gabriel heard her through but his face became sombre, almost grim.

"I see you have heard a lot of tales about me," he said bitterly. "But why do you come out with them now, when I ask you to marry me? You were kinder when you thought I had a wife living – when you offered to let me kiss you goodbye."

"Because it was goodbye," said Claudine, the anger in her beginning to turn into pain. "I was sorry for you."

"And why are you angry with me now?" he said, bewildered. "What has happened?"

"I don't know," said Claudine, with a sob, and turned

away, starting blindly down the path. She stumbled over a root.

Gabriel was close behind her. "Let me help you, please," he said, tentatively putting an arm across her shoulders.

"No!" Claudine shook him off and went on, determined, but hardly able to see through her tears.

A moment later they could see Thierry stopped on the path below, looking back. "We're coming!" called out Claudine.

Thierry waved and went on. Claudine pulled out a handkerchief and rubbed her eyes and her face. She must get control of herself; she must not let her agitation appear, especially to her mother.

"Claudine," Gabriel begged again, desperately, "don't leave me like this. What have I done wrong? Is it such an insult to love you?"

"Love! You don't love me," said Claudine, more fiercely than she realised, because she was so determined not to cry. "You don't know how to love, not what I call love. I wish you would leave me alone!"

Gabriel said nothing at all to that and as he was following behind her on the path, Claudine did not know how he looked. They went on in silence for a few moments till Claudine's hurried movement made her aware of something she had forgotten – his ring, on the chain with her medal.

"Oh, I nearly forgot to give you this," she said, stopping and pulling out the chain from her dress and fumbling hastily with the clasp, "which you used to trick me into seeing you, at Villerange."

She got the ring off the chain at last, nearly dropping the medal, and turned round to hold it out to him.

"Thank you," he said, taking it. "I shall feel its value much increased by knowing its hiding place."

Claudine fled again, muttering that it was there for convenience and safety. She thought he meant to tease her, and felt a dangerous softening towards him, within.

They were now coming down towards the hollow and the Temple was in sight. Gabriel was able to walk beside her and lengthened his stride to do so. Claudine thought of her mother's penetrating eye. "You won't say anything to my mother, will you?" she asked, anxiously.

"Indeed not," said Gabriel. "It was a mad impulse of mine, and I am punished for it, as I always am for acting on impulse." She was surprised at the bitterness in his voice. "I thought you had a kinder feeling for me than you have," he went on, more quietly, "I am sorry to have caused you distress by my mistake. But if the suddenness of my proposal made you feel it is insulting, please remember that I have to leave the country so soon. I could not resist making a snatch at the possibility of happiness which seemed to present itself. I realise now that it would be no sort of happiness to you, so be sure I will tease you no more. You need not run so fast away from me."

Claudine immediately found herself walking more slowly, but it was now too late for any more private conversation. Thierry and Seraphine were waiting by the Roman floor, which had to be covered up with a wooden structure that could not be shifted by one person. Thierry and Gabry moved it together, covering the broken mosiac of centaurs, beasts and birds, which had lain there so many hundreds of years, forgotten in the woods.

Soon after their return they had to leave to go home. Thierry and Gabriel escorted them down to the carriage; Thierry talked anxiously to Madame de Trévires about her brother's health, and whether he could stand a long journey; Gabry was almost entirely silent. He had put the ring on his hand.

Claudine felt restless and unhappy, she hardly knew why.

CHAPTER
ELEVEN

MADAME DE TRÉVIRES, who had never much liked her husband's enlightened modern school, decided over Christmas that she did not wish her daughters to return there.

"Claudine is quite bookish enough, and she is learning nothing of the world there," she told Gautier de Trévires. "I could see that Monsieur d'Erlen admired her – she is growing almost beautiful."

"Monsieur d'Erlen is the last man I should wish to admire a daughter of mine," observed Monsieur de Trévires dryly.

"Exactly, and she had no more idea how to deal with someone like him than she had at ten years old," said his wife, tartly.

"Well, but what can we do? If we take her to Luxembourg the French officers will fall in love with her," said Monsieur de Trévires. "I don't imagine that will please you any better than the admiration of the Comte de Villerange."

"I suggest we send her to my sister-in-law Charlotte de Lamerle, in Trèves," said Antoinette de Trévires. "Trèves is a big enough town to have some social life and Charlotte knows everybody there, since she was brought up in the place. She would take them out, and supervise them – for we could not send Claudine alone and Seraphine needs finishing as much as she does, for different reasons."

"Charlotte de Lamerle is a very respectable person, but she is a widow," objected Monsieur de Trévires. "If your eldest brother were still alive . . ."

"But *her* eldest brother is alive, the one who was a judge in the days of the Archbishop-Elector. They live in part of his house now."

Of course Antoinette de Trévires got her way; she usually did where the household affairs of Hautefontaine were concerned. Madame de Lamerle was written to, expressed herself delighted to take charge of her nieces for the rest of the winter, and almost before they had realised what was afoot

Claudine and Seraphine were sent, escorted by family servants, in the family carriage, to the ancient city of Trèves, or Trier as it was called by its German-speaking inhabitants.

It was hardly any distance away, just beyond the confluence of the Sûre and Moselle rivers, over what used to be the border between the duchy of Luxembourg and the Archbishopric of Trier. The girls had been there before the war and had visited the old churches and listened to their father's lectures on its history. But that was six or seven years ago, and at that time the Lamerle family were living at Solveringen, their home in Luxembourg. It was only when Constant de Lamerle had been killed, in '94, that his widow had retired to Trier, where she had been born, taking with her their only son, the last remaining male member of that family except for his Uncle Xavier, the priest.

Laurent de Lamerle was barely fifteen, and so Madame de Trévires did not anticipate any untoward love affairs between the cousins. She knew that her sister-in-law was a sensible woman of the world who, without strictness, would keep a careful watch over the two young girls.

Seraphine was in high spirits at the prospect and thought it only Claudine's quieter nature which prevented her from rejoicing likewise. But on the journey she thought her so melancholy that when they were stopped for a couple of hours to rest the horses, she asked her what was the matter.

"You seem to be thinking of something else all the time," she said.

"I am," said Claudine, with an impatient sigh.

Seraphine made an inspired guess. "Is it about the Comte de Villerange?"

Claudine admitted it, with a kind of groan. "I wish I could stop thinking about him," she said. "I don't mean to. I just can't help it."

"What happened on that walk beyond the Roman Temple?" asked Seraphine. "I thought you looked as if you had been crying."

"I don't know what to think of him," said Claudine. "He made me furious that day because he said if I would run away with him, he would marry me."

She was uneasily aware that this put the worst construction

on Gabriel's proposal, but she more than half believed it the true one.

Seraphine cried, "But he's married already!"

And when Claudine said that Gabriel had told her his wife was dead, she exclaimed. "I don't believe it!"

"He said that Thierry looks after his son because his wife had died," Claudine said doubtfully. She had, since Christmas, wondered much as to the truth of this statement.

"When he knew you couldn't ask Thierry!" said Seraphine. "Or mother, for then she would get suspicious. Oh, Claudine, you are very simple if you believe that! Rémy told us how he hates his wife. I think he is a brave fighter and splendid to look at, but everyone tells such stories of his behaviour to women. I am sure you should not trust him – certainly not to run away with him."

"Of course I never dreamt of doing that," said Claudine. "I told you, I was angry. I told him just what I thought of him."

"Was he annoyed?"

"He seemed not to understand why I was upset," answered Claudine. She hesitated. "I think he felt – disappointed. That's what I think now, I mean."

Seraphine laughed. "Of course he was disappointed! He must have thought you were ready to fall into his arms because you were so kind-hearted and look so innocent. Men never realise how determined you are – even papa doesn't."

"It wasn't only that kind of disappointment," said Claudine, more interested in Gabry's character than her own, "I can't explain, but I feel he expected me to be different."

"Well, you can't change yourself to please him," said Seraphine.

Claudine shook her head, but she could not understand her own feelings, let alone account for them to her sister.

"The trouble with you is that you can't leave things alone," said Seraphine. "Why should you worry about him? He'll go back across the Rhine and start making love to the German girls. He's probably forgotten about you already."

Although she felt she would have died rather than admit it,

this made Claudine feel more unhappy than any of her own thoughts on the subject. She did not want Gabry to forget her so soon; she resented those probable German girls. But neither did she want to be only another of the many girls he had loved.

The turmoil and intensity of her feelings made her a very passive visitor to Trier at first, but Madame de Lamerle did not notice it, since she remembered Claudine as the quiet one of the pair. Seraphine chattered for both and was soon teasing and being teased by her cousin Laurent, drawing attention to herself and away from her sister.

Laurent was about a year younger than Seraphine but he was already a little the taller, a slim boy with a thick cap of straight silky light-brown hair and a clear skin which increased the youthfulness of his appearance. This childlike clarity of countenance and his large grey blue eyes, fringed with long lashes, annoyed him very much, since his great wish was to be counted, as soon as possible, as a young man and not a boy. The only son of a widow, Laurent was anxious to prove himself manly and brave. His voice had not yet quite broken and though he tried to talk always in the deeper tone, he lost it as soon as he got excited, which he often did, in a childish treble.

Seraphine liked Laurent but could not resist teasing him; what began as argument frequently ended with their chasing each other round the house with shrieks of rage and laughter.

Madame de Lamerle lived in an apartment in her brother's big house, which stood on a corner of two streets in a central part of the town. There was a flight of paved stairs going up from the side street to a door on the first floor, where she had a suite of comfortable rooms. They had only to cross a landing to be in Judge Beck's house, but Charlotte de Lamerle had her own kitchen and servants, most of the Luxembourgers from her husband's small estate at Sol-veringen. These faithful retainers called Laurent "Seigneur" – which delighted him – but nevertheless ordered him about with privileged familiarity.

Although Johannes Beck was no longer a judge, having prudently retired when it became clear that the French were going to stay in Trier, he was still addressed as one and held in great respect. He was much older than his sister Charlotte and his large family were now dispersed, though one couple or another, with grandchildren, were usually staying in the big house with its high gabled roofs, and various members of older generations made their home there. The place seemed always full of people, solid, respectable good citizens, fond of music, conventionally but not fanatically religious, resentful of the French, but not inclined to defy them.

Laurent, whose father had been killed during the invasion, was a romantic patriot for Luxembourg and against the Revolution, sometimes alarming his mother by his wild outbursts. One of the family servants had recently come to Trier full of stories of the peasants' revolt in their district and Laurent could hardly bear it that he had not been at Solveringen to fight with them.

"As if they'd have let you – a boy of fifteen!" said Seraphine.

"They would have had to, because I am their seigneur," said Laurent proudly. "Besides, boys of my age have joined armies before now, so why not rebels?" It was particularly irritating to him because he had heard that other members of noble families had been involved. "Ernest Pelt says that one of the Erlens of Villerange has been leading a band of them round about Isenbourg, and some of our men joined him."

One of the Erlens of Villerange! It was impossible to get away from Gabry, it seemed to Claudine, or from the memory of him, since he himself must now be far away. They had heard from their mother that Uncle Xavier and "those others" had left Luxembourg on their way to the Rhine. That Gabry was among them Claudine guessed from her mother's remark that she could not be sorry that Gaston Ferrand was baulked of his prey.

Aunt Charlotte filled their days very thoroughly, with dancing lessons, needlework, practising on the pianoforte, and with taking them about among her acquaintance. She enjoyed having two pretty young nieces to plan for and immediately began speculating on suitors for Claudine, though she took care that she should not become fond of any young man not sufficiently well-born or well-endowed enough to please Antoinette de Trévires. But she soon began to think Claudine odd because she seemed not to notice the young men at the houses where they visited, but to be happy to listen to the old ones.

"Unawakened," said Charlotte de Lamerle to herself. "Childish, even though clever – just what one would expect from Gautier de Trévires' daughter."

She found Seraphine much easier to understand.

When the girls had arrived, Christmas festivities were still going on, and would indeed continue at least until Lent began. Seraphine was hoping they would be taken to a ball.

"What is the use of all the dancing lessons if we are never to dance?" she said.

They did get some impromptu dancing at evening visits, but it was not the same thing as a ball. Aunt Charlotte said there was to be a public ball to which she thought she might safely take them, but it was not until February.

January was now fairly advanced and the weather was cold; snow crusted the roofs of the old town and picked out the Gothic detail on ancient churches, some of them closed, others allowed to function in a subdued way under the care of priests who had taken the oath to the constitution and often married a wife as well: pious lay people considered these equal delinquencies. Trier, like most ecclesiastical provinces, had an anti-clerical faction and these people had welcomed the French Republic. Judge Beck managed to remain neutral.

One day about noon Madame de Lamerle and her nieces were coming back on foot from an expedition to buy new ribbons and trimmings, when Claudine saw, some way ahead of them and walking in the same direction, a tall man in a long greatcoat and wearing a high-crowned round-brimmed hat, pushed to the back of his head. Her heart gave a jump; for a moment she thought it was Gabriel d'Erlen.

Then she was annoyed with herself. Gabry must be well on his way to the Rhine by now, if not over it, and in any case he did not wear clothes like that, gentleman's clothes, while he was hiding from the French. What was more, the tall citizen of Trier was walking arm in arm with his wife, and, she noticed, when some people in between them shifted aside, he had a child swinging on his other hand, a little girl of five or six.

"He is not the only tall man in the world," she told herself.

All the same, she could not help watching the trio ahead.

The woman was talking, turning her head sideways and up to her companion, so that Claudine could see her profile, and see, too, that she was smiling with pleasure. She was a fair woman, perhaps about thirty, not beautiful, but pretty in a homely way and with a shapely figure; she was dressed simply but quite well and the child wore a fur-trimmed cape and a little bonnet.

"I suppose he has been away as they are making such a fuss of him," Claudine thought.

And then the man turned his head to look at the woman and Claudine felt a shock like a blow on the midriff. She could not mistake that eagle profile. It *was* Gabry.

He was wearing such a high-collared coat that from behind the scar on his cheek was not visible; nevertheless she was certain it was he. And as they went on and he later looked down, from time to time, either at the woman or the little girl, there was no doubt of it. He never looked around enough to notice anyone behind him and indeed they were so far behind that Claudine wondered if Seraphine had seen him at all; she was chattering away to her aunt.

But what could Gabry be doing in Trier? Why had he stayed behind, so near Luxembourg, instead of helping Thierry to get Xavier de Lamerle safely over the Rhine? To see this woman? And who was she? She seemed to know Gabry very well and yet to Claudine's eye she did not look sufficiently well-born to be any sort of relation of his. She was dressed, and she moved, like a good bourgeoise.

Suddenly the trio ahead turned off down a side-street and as they passed the end of it Claudine glanced furtively down, but saw no one. She was still brooding over it when they reached the Judge's house.

As soon as they were in their bedroom Seraphine exclaimed, "Claudine! Did you see him? Monsieur d'Erlen! In Trèves!"

"Yes, I saw him," said Claudine, taking off her hat and beginning to brush her hair in front of the glass. Her own face looked pale and blank to her. "I wondered what on earth he was doing here."

Seraphine said, "Well, evidently he hasn't come to look for you but that woman he was with."

"Do you think so?" Claudine tried to speak casually.

"Of course she's one of his mistresses from the old days,"

said Seraphine, who was always ready with a story of explanation for people's actions. "You know what a lot of *émigrés* were here before the invasion."

"But she doesn't look French," said Claudine, "or like the nobility who fled from the Revolution."

"Oh no, but she might have been a maid of one of them," said Seraphine. "You know the Marquise, whose child was supposed to be his? She came here to have it. This woman could have been her maid then."

"But if the Marquise was his mistress he could hardly have had an affair with her maid as well," objected Claudine, caught, as usual, into Seraphine's inventive imagination.

Seraphine giggled. "Perhaps later – because you know Victoire says the Marquise threw him over for another man."

"So you talked to Victoire about him, too?" said Claudine.

She sat down to change her shoes, anxious to hide her face from her sister's bright-eyed inquisitive gaze.

"Of course I did, though there was not much time," said Seraphine. "Besides, that little girl – didn't you see what dark curls she had? Quite unlike her mother! She's probably another of his children."

Claudine's wonderings had not gone as far as that.

"Really, Seraphine, what a little scandal-monger you are!"

"Well – but can you deny that they did not appear very familiar with each other?" asked Seraphine. "And delighted to meet again."

Claudine could not deny it.

"It's just as well to have seen it," she said. "One has heard enough of these women of his, but it is not real till one has seen one of them in person."

Something in her tone made Seraphine say, "You don't mind, Claudine, do you? You refused to run away with him, after all."

"Why should I mind?" said Claudine.

But she was glad to hear her aunt's voice, calling them downstairs.

The trouble was that she did mind, very much. She thought of that time in the lobby, when Gabry would not kiss her because it was a beginning and not an end; she thought of him in the woods above the Roman floor, saying he wanted to marry her more than anything in the world. And then she saw him again in her mind's eye, smiling at the pretty fair woman on his arm, holding the hand of that dark-haired child, who might perhaps be his own.

"He's just not someone to be trusted," she thought sadly. In spite of that, she knew she was longing to see him again.

CHAPTER
TWELVE

NEXT day, in the wintry afternoon, Claudine was sitting in her cold bedroom by the window to catch the dim light on her book, but at last it became too dark to see and she reluctantly threw off the quilt she had wrapped herself in for warmth and went down from the second to the first floor, walking straight into the drawing-room, for she did not expect anyone but her aunt and her sister to be there.

The lamp was lighted, the room was warm and glowing, and sitting in a chair near the stove was her cousin Thierry.

Claudine stopped still in astonishment. Thierry was dressed in the clothes he had worn on first coming to Hautefontaine, the ordinary clothes of a professional man, plain and drab, but not the peasant's gear in which she had last seen him.

Thierry smiled at her. "I expect you are as surprised to see me as I was to see Seraphine," he said, "and I am afraid it is a sad reason which has brought me to see Aunt Charlotte. Uncle Xavier had such a severe attack, coughing blood, on our journey, that I decided we must stop here in Trèves and see a good physician. I came to consult Madame about that."

"Of course I wanted to fetch Xavier here at once," said Charlotte de Lamerle. "But Thierry does not think it would be fair to the Judge to bring an escaped prisoner under his roof."

"I can look after him very well where we are," said Thierry. "It is a respectable lodging, and the woman who keeps it is good and trustworthy."

Of course the girls wanted to visit their uncle at once, but Thierry was evasive, and finally arranged to come next day and escort them there. Claudine could not help wondering if it was because Gabry was there too, with that fair woman and her child. Seraphine was sure of it. "I expect she keeps the lodgings," was her guess.

But though they did indeed go into the side-street which

Claudine had seen Gabriel enter, the woman who opened the door to them was about fifty, with plain heavy features and hair dyed black. Frau Hannah Müller had given up one of her own ground-floor rooms to the sick priest and was helping to nurse him. As Thierry took them to it, a girl came out with a cup in her hand. It was Lisel.

"Lisel!" cried Seraphine in astonishment. "What are you doing here?"

Lisel blushed crimson. "Oh, mademoiselle! I am going abroad with – with Monsieur de Ravanger. I have married – one of his servants." She seemed very confused, and slipped away, down the stairs to the basement.

"Lisel is embarrassed because she had to get married in such a hurry in order to come with us," said Thierry, smiling. "Uncle Xavier performed the ceremony, so it is a good church marriage, even if it is not a civil one!"

Then he took them into the back bedroom.

As soon as she saw her uncle, Claudine thought sadly, "He is going to die."

A few moments later, after he had been talking to them, she could not have said why she had thought that – the first impression faded. He seemed even thinner than he had been a month ago at Christmas, but his eyes were still alive and bright, and his voice, though weak and hoarse, quite cheerful.

"I want Thierry to go, and leave me here," he said, "but he won't."

"Of course not," said Thierry. "And Aunt Charlotte is full of good advice. We shall have you up again soon, *mon cher oncle*."

Presently Madame de Lamerle sent the two girls out of the room and they went into the small front parlour, where Frau Müller had put out some cups and a jug of coffee. As they sat there, with the door to the hall open, sipping their coffee in subdued silence, suddenly the street door opened and they heard a child's voice, quickly hushed by a woman's.

"Ssh, Paulette! Don't forget the poor gentleman ill in bed."

She spoke in German.

"I smell coffee!" the child said in her loud whisper and looked in at the door and then, seeing two strange young ladies, ran out again.

Claudine saw the dark curls and piquant little face of the child she had seen holding Gabriel's hand, the day before yesterday. And the woman who hurried her away up the stairs was the fair woman who had walked arm in arm with him.

Seraphine looked across at her sister. "They are lodgers here!" she murmured, raising her eyebrows.

Claudine said nothing. She felt certain now that Gabry was staying here too, and that Thierry did not want her to know it. Or perhaps it was Gabry who did not want her to know it?

Presently Aunt Charlotte and Thierry came in and discussed doctors and treatment over their coffee. Frau Müller brought in some home-made biscuits and watched them all with shrewd curiosity. When it was time to leave Madame de Lamerle refused to allow Thierry to accompany them.

"We are no distance from home," she assured him, as she went down the steps, and summoned her nieces to walk one each side.

It was as they turned out of the side street into the main road that they met Gabriel d'Erlen, who was just about to enter it.

"Claudine!" he said, using her christian name in his surprise.

Madame de Lamerle fixed him with a piercing glance. "Do you know this gentleman, Claudine?" she demanded sternly.

"Y – Yes, aunt," Claudine said nervously, "I have met him with my mother."

Gabriel bowed and said, "If you are Claudine's aunt, Madame, I may introduce myself as Thierry de Ravanger's cousin."

"Why, you must be one of the Erlens of Villerange," said Madame de Lamerle. "Indeed, you have the look of that family."

"Yes, Madame, but I would prefer you to call me Paul Gabry, which is the name on my papers," he replied. "And are your nieces staying with you here? That is very good news."

Madame de Lamerle looked as if she was not sure that it was good news that he knew it. She was plainly recalling all the stories about the young Comte de Villerange.

Gabriel, however, appeared quite at ease. He turned to

accompany them home, walking on the further side of Claudine.

"Thierry never told me you were here," he said. "Or did he not know himself till today?"

Claudine, not knowing how to answer this, asked how long he intended to stay in Trier.

It appeared that this depended on Xavier de Lamerle's health, since Gabry meant to stay with his cousin till they crossed the Rhine.

"Though he swears he is better off without me," he said cheerfully. "But Norbert and Lisel are useful to him, even if I'm not, and Norbert would never stay if I went."

"Norbert and Lisel?" echoed Claudine, wondering at their names being thus linked.

"Yes – we discovered that old Norbert was dying for love," said Gabriel, with a chuckle. "And Lisel was willing to leave home for his sake, so we had a wedding at the Roman Temple before we left. Wenzel, her brother, gave her away – rather to my disappointment, as I was hoping to do it myself. However, I was Norbert's best man instead."

"And didn't miss kissing the bride, I expect," said Seraphine pertly.

Gabry laughed; he did not seem to mind this piece of naughtiness from Claudine's little sister, though Aunt Charlotte looked shocked.

Claudine herself could not help wondering if that was the kind of wedding he had meant to offer her, and not an elopement with a possible marriage at the end of it. The supposition made her silent.

When they reached the side door of the Judge's house, Madame de Lamerle invited Gabry upstairs. She had evidently decided that, reputation for gallantry or no, the Comte de Villerange was not someone her late husband would have wished her to slight.

On the landing they met Laurent, just released by his tutor from the lessons which he took in the Judge's library. He had come leaping and bounding and whistling through the door connecting the two parts of the house and stopped dead at the sight of the tall stranger with the scarred face.

"My son, Laurent, monsieur," said Madame de Lamerle.

"He looks a fine fellow," said Gabriel, "worthy to be the son of Constant de Lamerle."

Laurent smiled with delight at such a greeting.

"Did you know my father, monsieur?"

"Certainly, and when I was your age he was very good to me," said Gabriel. "He understood better than anyone what I felt like when I found my foolishness had lamed my cousin for life – his nephew Thierry, of whom he was very fond."

Charlotte de Lamerle looked keenly at him. "That must have been just before I married him," she said. "But I did not see much of you, monsieur, in your youthful days. I suppose it was because you were so soon away with the Austrian army."

"It's possible Monsieur de Lamerle thought I had turned out badly, in spite of his kindness," said Gabriel. "Many people did – still do, no doubt."

At that moment a servant came to take his coat. It was Ernest Pelt from Solveringen, and he broke out excitedly in dialect, "Ah, Monsieur le Comte! How glad I am to see you safe and sound! We heard that the French had caught you, down at Villerange."

"So they did, but my men rescued me before I got to Luxembourg," said Gabry, smiling. "Well, Ernst! I didn't expect to see you here. How is your brother? Did he have to lose that arm of his?"

"He did, monsieur, but after all, it is not such a tragedy, for as his wife says, the French will not want to take a one-armed man," said Ernest. "So he will never have to fight in the revolutionary army."

Laurent, who had been listening and eagerly looking from one to the other, now burst out, "But are you the Comte d'Erlen who has been fighting with our people up at Solveringen?"

"Yes – though we have failed, as you probably know, boy," said Gabry. "It is sickening to learn that now, when it is too late, Austria is again at war with France. I am on my way to join the Archduke Charles."

"Oh," cried Laurent, "let me come with you!"

"Laurent," said his mother, "don't be ridiculous. Monsieur d'Erlen does not want a boy of fifteen on his hands."

"But how much older was he, when he joined the army, as you said just now he did?" Laurent demanded.

"Not much, but a little," said Gabry, with a smile. "I was sixteen and I went as aide-de-camp to my own father;

nor were we at war then, so you see it was not quite the same."

Madame de Lamerle now succeded in getting them into the drawing room but Ernest, sent to fetch wine, came back with several other Luxembourgeois servants, all eager to see Gabriel and ask him about friends and relations who had gone south with him to Villerange. Aunt Charlotte saw that she must allow him to answer their questions, which he did straightforwardly; he did not seem at a loss for anyone's name and family. Laurent sat on a stool, fascinated.

But at last Madame de Lamerle sent the servants away, with a reminder that they must not speak of Monsieur le Comte de Villerange by his name.

"What did you say your assumed name was?" she asked.

"Paul Gabry, and my profession, for the benefit of the French, is instructor in arms," said Gabry, smiling. "It has to be! It's the only thing I know anything about. But as it happens I know a good fellow here who keeps a small fencing school, so I have someone to vouch for me, if necessary."

"Oh, I wish you would teach me!" said Laurent. "Since I had to leave school, I've had *nothing*." He glanced accusingly at his mother.

"Of course I could not let him go to school with republicans and be taught atheism," said Madame de Lamerle. "When the college was closed, I had a tutor come here for Laurent."

"But he knows absolutely nothing about fighting," said Laurent.

"So much the better," his mother said tartly. "In any case, fencing is hardly a preparation for modern warfare, is it, monsieur?"

"Perhaps not, but it's a very good exercise," replied Gabry. "It might be good for Monsieur Laurent – teach him not to throw his arms and legs about so carelessly!"

Laurent flushed and laughed; he knew he was restless.

"Monsieur de Lamerle was a very good swordsman," said Gabriel, with his eye on the boy. "He taught Thierry – who was twice as good as me, before his leg was broken. If you like, Madame, I could introduce your son to Gustave Thills, who is not in the least of the republican persuasion."

Laurent leapt up, excited, and begged his mother's permission There was some discussion which ended in Madame

de Lamerle's agreeing to go next morning with Gabriel to the
fencing master's rooms.

"And us too!" cried Seraphine. "I should like to see it so
much."

"It is not a grand school, you know," Gabry said. "Gustave has only one room and lives above it. He is proficient
enough to take a better position, but he will not leave Trèves
so long as his old mother is alive."

Soon afterwards Madame de Lamerle invited him to dine,
as the dinner hour was approaching. But then he rose at once
to leave, saying that Thierry was expecting him. "And if I
don't turn up he will think I have fallen foul of the French
police, though I am sure no one in Trèves has ever heard of
Le Cicatrisé – except your good servants, Madame."

He was going, and Claudine had not said a word to him for
the whole of his visit, or he to her directly, though he had
been looking at her often enough. And when he said goodbye
he called her "Mademoiselle" and not by her name, as in the
first moment of surprise.

Aunt Charlotte had nothing to complain of in his conduct.
After he had gone she said, "He is a much easier man to know
than his father – probably because he has a sense of humour. I
can't imagine Constant's liking him, if he had not. I
remember him speaking of Gabriel sometimes, when we
were first married."

"What did he say of him?" Seraphine asked, and Claudine
thought how useful it was to have an inquisitive sister. It was
just what she wanted to know.

"Oh, he said Gabry was a high-spirited boy, impulsive and
quick-tempered, and over-confident of himself, but not
domineering, like so many of his family. Constant said that
after that accident to his cousin he hardly knew what to do
with himself for remorse, and his father only made it worse,
by blaming him all the time in front of everyone. I can quite
believe dear Constant helped him to come to terms with his
guilt – he was always a person of much understanding for
others."

At dinner, while the talk flowed round her, Claudine was
silent, thinking of Gabriel d'Erlen. It was very strange, this
meeting him again a month after she had imagined she had
parted with him for ever – and parted in anger, at that. She
had scarcely spoken to him and yet in that short time she

seemed to have discovered a whole new dimension of his life, what might be called the ordinary side of it.

It was emphasised for her by the fact that, for the first time since she had met him, he was wearing the ordinary dress of a gentleman, and though the clothes were chosen to be inconspicuous they fitted much too well not to be his own. She realised that he must have come into French territory dressed like this, as "Paul Gabry, instructor of arms", and the clothes had been kept somewhere, to be resumed when the year of rebel life was over. But to see him in tail-coat and close-fitting pantaloons, looking not merely clean but well-groomed, made him seem almost a different person and certainly a more respectable one. Claudine was rather ashamed that a mere change in dress should make such an alteration in her attitude, but so it was.

Gabry in rough peasant's dress, a rebel on the run, had been someone easy to imagine oneself in love with but such as to make talk of marriage sound utterly insincere on his lips. But Monsieur d'Erlen, Count of Villerange, talking to her aunt, taking an interest in young Laurent's education, someone with family connections like anyone else, seemed much less likely to have intended a mere seduction.

But that was quite illogical! For not even Thierry had denied that Gabry's morals were unreliable; Thierry had said the story about the Marquise was true. And she herself had seen him walking arm-in-arm with that fair woman, with the little dark-haired girl called Paulette. Paulette! And *Paul* Gabry! Claudine hardened her heart.

"He can't care much for me, if he has gone straight back to her," she told herself firmly.

CHAPTER
THIRTEEN

LAURENT DE LAMERLE was dancing with impatience by the time Gabry turned up next morning; he had been ready early and Gabry arrived later than he had said, with no better excuse than that he had not noticed the time.

Gustave Thills, the fencing master, had a long room with a boarded floor, and when they entered it he was putting his half-dozen pupils through a series of basic positions. He was a wiry man with a springy walk and thick hair cut short to his head like stiff fur. He came hurrying to greet them and bowed as elegantly as a dancing master.

Laurent was relieved to see two boys of his own age – the others were all a few years older and bigger. The ladies were shown to chairs where they could sit and watch.

"But you, monsieur, you must not sit!" said Gustave Thills to Gabry. "I have told my pupils that now we shall have the chance to demonstrate to them the various thrusts and parries in action."

"What! You want me to make a fool of myself in front of the ladies?" said Gabriel, laughing. "My dear Gustave, I haven't had a foil in my hand for over a year. I am quite out of practice."

"It will soon come back to you," said the fencing master confidently. "Skill such as yours, monsieur, is not really lost."

"Flatterer!" said Gabriel. "Well, let me go through some exercises with the boys, first."

He stripped off his coat and Gustave Thills lent him a padded white jacket. In some places masks had begun to be used, but he did not possess them, explaining to Laurent's anxious mother that the target was on the chest, and he did not allow the boys to fight each other.

The girls watched the exercises with interest, and still more the demonstration of a proper match between Thills and Gabriel. They had never seen any fencing before because

their father disapproved of it as a mere preparation for duel-
ling – though nowadays duels were generally fought out with
pistols.

"I see what Gabry meant about Laurent learning to control
his arms and legs," said Seraphine presently. "It needs even
more balance and discipline than dancing."

The movements were so formalised as to give the appearance of a ritual dance, and yet the skill lay in outwitting the
opponent by what seemed to the girls an infinite series of
tricks.

Gabriel was perhaps too tall to make a perfect fencer,
but he had a steady wrist and a good balance. He was
better in attack than in defence, which did not surprise
Claudine.

Towards the end, Thierry de Ravanger walked in, with his
quick limping gait, and came to sit with his cousins.

"I thought old Gustave would get Gabry working!" he
remarked, with a smile.

He was able to explain the points and rules of the game,
which Seraphine wanted to understand. Claudine was quite
content simply to watch. She was aware, as she had been that
day at the Roman Temple, of Gabry's masculine physical
grace, the apparent ease of his control, and effortless energy,
and suddenly she wished she could dance with him. She had
temporarily forgotten that she did not intend to allow herself
to take notice of him.

After the demonstration Laurent was to be initiated in the
first steps of the art and Gabriel came back to the seats,
laughing and pulling on his coat.

"It's too bad of you, Thierry, to come and watch my
mistakes!" he said. "You know, he is really much more an
expert than I."

Claudine thought of that business of the wall; she saw that
Gabriel could never forget it.

Presently Madame de Lamerle remembered it was time for
Seraphine to go to the dressmaker to be fitted for her ball-
dress. Claudine's was already nearly finished but their aunt
had not at first intended her younger niece to attend the ball,
and when she had yielded to Seraphine's frantic pleading, the
dress had to be hurriedly made.

"We will come back for Laurent," said Madame de
Lamerle. "You had better come with us, Claudine."

"Must I?" said Claudine. "It is so dull at the dress-maker's."

"Let me take you to see the Porta Nigra, *chère cousine*," said Thierry, "the old Roman Gate, into which our Christian ancestors built all sorts of oddities."

Aunt Charlotte allowed this, when she saw that Gabriel d'Erlen was staying in the fencing school. But Thierry and Claudine had not got very far when Gabry caught them up.

"A sudden interest in antiquarian buildings, Gabry?" Thierry teased him. He had Claudine's arm in his, and Gabriel fell into step beside her.

"After living so many weeks in a Roman Temple even I must become a classic," he said cheerfully.

They walked towards the ancient gate, Claudine trying to remember what her father had told her about it and Thierry, as usual, full of stories of the human beings probably or improbably connected with it.

Gabry, after saying that he had never thought about it as a building before, remarked that it would look better if some-one knocked off all the mediaeval excrescences.

"But that would knock off half the stories too," said "What would Cousin Thierry do then?"

"Invent them – as he has probably invented these," said Gabry. "Though I am sure it would be rash to try to deceive the daughter of Gautier de Trévires! Especially when she has stayed at school so long!"

His tone was teasing, but Claudine did not mind.

"We weren't allowed to read half the books in your lib-rary," she said.

"I should think not!" said Gabriel. "My grandfather was a scabrous old character who would pay any money to get books about people doing what they should not. All bound in heavy calf with false titles in Latin. Your virtuous cousin Thierry found that out, I may say."

"I wonder if Madame Bilsdorf has discovered them?" said Thierry. "I don't believe your father knew they were there, Gabry."

"My dear fellow, father always preferred the flesh to the word," said Gabriel, and then hastily apologized to Claudine for using such an expression. "Living in the woods for a year has turned me into a savage," he said, looking, as he said it, extremely civilised.

In fact, it interested Claudine that as soon as he was out of the woods, Gabriel obviously took some trouble with his appearance. In spite of the necessity of looking like a mere instructor of arms there was about him something of the grand manner that suggested instead his actual descent from a long line of military seigneurs. She remembered, suddenly, the picture at Villerange, which showed him as a handsome boy of fifteen, swaggering with his gun and his dog, and it amused her.

"What are you smiling at, Concordia?" he said, watching her expression.

"You!" she replied boldly. "The noble savage!"

Gabry was delighted at this retort and laughed with pleasure at having elicited it from her.

Claudine was so much enjoying this walk that a sudden change in the emotional climate came as a shock. It happened when Gabry discovered, from something Thierry said, that his cousin had known the girls to be in Trier and had not only not told him, but had tried to arrange their visit to Xavier de Lamerle to coincide with his absence.

It was the first time Claudine had seen any sign of the quick temper Gabriel was said to have.

"*Mon dieu*, Thierry! That is a bit too much!" he said, stopping still, and his eyes looked much greener than usual with the flash of anger.

"I did it to save Claudine embarrassment," Thierry returned firmly. "Because I knew she had been upset by your behaviour at Villerange."

"What do you know about that? You know nothing!" Gabriel said furiously, speaking over Claudine's head.

"I know because she told me," said Thierry. "And I was not at all sure you had not taken advantage of that walk above the Roman Temple to annoy her again."

"You damned interfering prig!" said Gabry, between his teeth.

Claudine felt that if she had not been between them he might even have struck his cousin; she saw his fist clench.

"Oh – please don't quarrel," she said anxiously. "Please not."

"It's you, I suppose, who told her all that nonsense about me," said Gabriel to Thierry, hardly noticing her interruption.

"Gabry, be calm," said Thierry, who was not himself excited. "If you think about it, you'll see I acted for Claudine's interest as I saw it. But now that you have met again, it is up to you to prove you can behave honourably if you choose."

Glancing up at Gabriel, Claudine saw that this sudden rage had carried away his self-control. He was much too angry to say anything peaceable, but just managed to prevent himself from speaking at all. He gave her a quick bow and walked rapidly away from them.

Claudine felt very much shaken; she was trembling, and Thierry noticed it. "My poor girl! I am sorry about this," he said. "Come, sit down here."

He led her to a bench outside a tavern. "This is perhaps not the most suitable place to sit, but probably you will not be noticed."

Claudine sat down.

"I am sorry I provoked Gabry like that," Thierry said. "I hope his rage didn't frighten you? It goes off quite quickly."

Claudine felt hypocritical. Gabriel's burst of temper had not frightened her at all; but it had made her realise the strength of his feeling for herself. He was angry with frustration, because Thierry had reinforced the bad character which he knew had been the cause of her refusal to listen to him, that time at Christmas. In fact, his anger made her feel sympathetic to him.

"Thierry," she said suddenly, "is his wife alive?"

Thierry was obviously surprised at this sudden and apparently inconsequent question.

"No, she died over a year ago, in England," he said. "I thought you knew that. Ludovic, his son, has lived with me since then."

"That's what he said, but I wasn't sure if it was true," said Claudine. "You see, when we went up the hill to look at the ruins he asked me to marry him – to go across the Rhine with him. At first I thought he was mocking me and afterwards I thought perhaps – perhaps he was intending to – to deceive me. Of course I could not marry him, even if he meant it. I know how he behaved to his wife, Victoire told me. And you said it was true he had a child by that mistress of his, the Marquise."

Thierry was evidently much surprised by this history.

"No wonder he was angry with me just now," he said. "Of course I did not know he had asked you to marry him."

"You think he really meant it, then?" asked Claudine.

"My dear little cousin, that is the one thing he would mean, if he asked it," said Thierry seriously. "His marriage was such that he once told me that even if he were free he would never marry again. At that time, he was certainly cynical about women, and that's why I was worried about you, Claudine. But perhaps I have wronged him; he must have fallen very much in love with you."

"But he hardly knows me," said Claudine.

Thierry smiled. When he smiled his wide mouth made heavy creases in his thin cheeks. His grey eyes were gleaming under the heavy lids.

"Well, love is an unpredictable thing," he said. "And Gabry is a headlong, impulsive fellow who can't imagine he won't get what he wants, if he tries hard enough for it. Evidently he hasn't given up hope, in spite of your refusal."

Claudine got up. "Let's walk home now," she said. "And I wish you would tell me something about that wife of his. Victoire said he married for more property and then insulted her by having an affair with this Marquise, in their own home at Villerange."

"Well, that's half the truth," said Thierry, picking up his stick and giving her his arm.

They walked slowly back through the ancient city, past tall gabled houses and baroque palaces, past Gothic church and Roman basilica – Constantine's judgement hall – so that their images were imprinted on Claudine's mind as she listened to the story of Gabry's marriage, told by his cousin.

"It was the parents who made the match," he said. "Anne-Louise de Gaudray was the heiress of Rehoncourt, just over the border in France. She agreed to please her father, for whom she had the most complete admiration. She was twenty, the same age as Gabriel, though she seemed older, for she was a cool, clever young woman. Probably she ought to have married someone much older than herself – certainly not a hotheaded young daredevil, as Gabry was in those days, with so much energy to spare that he would do mad things just for a bet. She wasn't beautiful and when he first saw her he didn't like her – I am not sure that dislike at first sight is not even more common than love at first sight!"

"But he married her," said Claudine.

"Yes, to please his mother, my good aunt, who was in a decline and dying," said Thierry. "There had been a fuss not long before over a maidservant who went to the Comtesse with a tale of seduction."

"Oh yes, Victoire mentioned that too," said Claudine.

Thierry glanced at her; he was evidently a little surprised at her matter-of-fact tone. Seraphine would have said that, like all men, he had been taken in by Claudine's innocent look, imagining her more of a child than she was.

"Well, I think that girl was quite as much sinning as sinned against," he said, with a smile, "but my aunt thought Gabry might be saved from a dissolute life by an early marriage. Poor Aunt Marie-Madeleine! Perhaps it was a mercy she did not live to see how things turned out – she died just after Ludovic was born, the year before the Revolution began in Paris. I am sure she did not realise that the marriage was a failure, for Gabry was away so much and Anne-Louise far too proud to complain. Perhaps she had no complaint to make, for she married the heir of Villerange rather than someone called Gabry – and she never called him that, even in private. He was Monsieur d'Erlen always.

"She was a formal person, cold by nature, and did not enjoy good health. The doctors did not think she ought to have more children and both of them were content to live apart. So you see it was not much of a marriage when the Marquise arrived on the scene, fleeing from the Revolution, very pretty and pathetic and longing for love, for the poor girl had been married off at sixteen to an old man. He had hoped for an heir, but after five years they had no child and he was even older. Well, what must that idiot Gabriel do but fall madly in love with her, so madly that everybody for miles around knew what was going on."

"Her husband too?" said Claudine.

"Certainly," said Thierry. "But poor fellow, what with his gout and his liver, and the loss of all his property, he was quite ready to look the other way. Only when Madame became pregnant he brought her here to Trier. This is where Gilles was born, in the winter of '91."

"Gilles is Gabry's illegitimate son?" said Claudine.

"Yes, and it's plain enough from his looks," said Thierry. "If there were lands in question I imagine the Marquis's family would have made a case of it, but at present the boy is still known by his name – d'Ivranches. I see him sometimes, as his mother has married a rich English lord. The poor old Marquis died almost as soon as they arrived in England."

"She didn't marry Gabriel," observed Claudine.

"A milord in the hand is worth two *émigrés* in the bush!" said Thierry, with a smile. "Besides, Anne-Louise was alive then. And Gabry was out of love with the Marquise in any case – she threw him over in favour of a French aristocrat when she was here in Trèves. Hence his cynicism, and hence my fears for you, *chère cousine*, though I did not quite believe Gabriel would try to seduce a young unmarried girl."

Claudine walked on in silence and presently Thierry said, "Perhaps you think I have not improved Gabry's character by telling you all this? But I want you to understand that the failure of his marriage was not all his fault. And I think it made Madame less unhappy than it made Monsieur, because she was a person who could do without love, but he isn't."

"No, I am glad to know more about it, and that he was not so cold-heartedly selfish as old Victoire made out," said Claudine, gravely. "Of course, she hates men – we used to laugh about it at school."

"Gabry could never be cold-hearted about anything," said Thierry. "His trouble is that his blood is too hot! But I am afraid he has not shown himself a model of constancy, so I think you were right to refuse his sudden proposal, even though he must have meant all that he said at the time."

They arrived at the Judge's house and Thierry left Claudine at the door, to go back to his uncle.

He was to come back in the evening and stay for supper; Madame de Lamerle had invited Gabriel too, but only Thierry turned up, apologising for his cousin's absence. "I haven't seen him since this morning," he said, with a glance at Claudine.

Charlotte de Lamerle, who was fond of music, asked Thierry to play to them, and they sat in the lamplit room, while he played sonatas by Haydn and Mozart on the pianoforte. Claudine was still thinking about the morning's conversation. While it helped her to understand Gabriel better, it was not exactly encouraging to learn that he was given to falling violently in and out of love. "How long will it last with me?" she wondered.

And there was always the memory of that woman at the lodging house. Although Claudine could speak easily enough of the Marquise, whose affair with Gabriel had taken place when she herself had been a child of ten, she was far too shy to say anything to Thierry about this other woman and her little girl.

Thierry had begun a sonata by Mozart when Ernest Pelt came in and told her, in a deferential whisper, that she was wanted outside. Thinking it was one of the old aunts who haunted the household and were always calling on her services, Claudine got up with resignation and followed Ernest to the landing.

But then he turned to her and whispered, "Monsieur d'Erlen wants to see you, mademoiselle. He is waiting on the stairs from the street. He asked me to beg you to come, just for a few moments."

Claudine nodded, and went, rather slowly, to the head of the flight that led down to the street. Ernest Pelt tiptoed discreetly off towards the backstairs. Evidently his admiration for Monsieur d'Erlen as a rebel leader led him to obey his every command.

Claudine paused at the top of the stairs and looked down. The lamp on the landing illuminated her, in her white dress, with her heavy gold-brown locks on her bare neck. Gabriel was standing in the shadow below, in his long greatcoat with the high collar, so that his face, looking up, was the most visible part of him.

He said something, as she appeared, that she could not hear.

"What did you say, monsieur?" she asked, descending a few steps.

Mozart sounded in the air – quick, delicate rhythms of sound.

Gabry came up the stairs towards her but stopped where he was still in the shadow. "You look like a Florentine angel, on one of those heavenly ladders," he said.

Claudine smiled, looking more like one than ever. She went down a few more steps. "Ernest said you wished to speak to me," she said. "But we were expecting you this evening."

"I know, and I have been walking about this hour, trying to make up my mind what to do," said Gabriel. "In the end I decided I must see you first, Claudine. If you really feel such a dislike of meeting me as Thierry suggested this morning, I could not come into this house. Somehow I thought you did not, when we met again – so unexpectedly. But I can't forget what you said to me, last Christmas day, in the woods at Villerange. No doubt Thierry knows you better than I do."

"But he didn't know anything about that," Claudine said. "All he knew about was that time when I ran into you in the passage – and I was cross, because you didn't seem to care what I felt, then, only what you felt. You must not be angry with Thierry, he has been defending you."

"You saw how angry I was," said Gabriel despondently. "I thought I'd grown out of those stupid rages but it seems I haven't. Thierry was right to try to protect you against me. Several times today I almost decided to go away and leave you in peace. But somehow I couldn't, or not without seeing you again, just once."

Claudine was silent. There were many good reasons why she should now be cool and tell him to go away, but none of them was strong enough to overcome her desire that he should not.

Because she said nothing, Gabriel presently began again.

"I know it was wrong – it was selfish – to want to carry you off beyond the Rhine, away from your family," he said. "I promise I won't try to persuade you to do that. But the war won't last for ever. When the Archduke has beaten the French . . ." He did not end the sentence but stood looking up at her and then suddenly broke out, "Claudine! Tell me Thierry was wrong. You don't hate the sight of me, do you?"

It was not a confident demand but an almost desperate request for reassurance.

Claudine's defences, already shaken, collapsed altogether.

"Oh no," she said, coming down another step, so that their faces were almost on a level. "I was pleased to see you again, Gabry."

"Were you?" he said eagerly, taking her hand.

"I think I was unfair to you, when I didn't believe what you said, that time in the woods," Claudine went on hurriedly. "Thierry said you would not have asked me to – to marry you if you had not meant it."

"Did he?" enquired Gabriel. "Then perhaps I'll forgive him for suggesting that I was some kind of provincial Don Juan, not to be trusted alone with any girl."

He moved up to the step just below the one where she was standing, so that because of his height he stood a little higher than she did. "So, Claudine," he said gently, "so long as I don't say 'fly with me!', you won't object to a friendly acquaintance, while we are both in Trier?"

Claudine shook her head and smiled. "I won't object," she repeated.

It was a soft, breathless reply. For now that they were so close, and now that Gabry had her hand in his, she suddenly felt a strong desire for his embrace – just what she had shied away from before. It was more than she had felt in the lobby at Villerange, when she had naïvely suggested that he might kiss her because he was going away. Because this time it was not merely a question of being kissed. She wanted to kiss him too.

So perhaps it was not surprising that this was what happened, hardly a moment after he had been saying that a friendly acquaintance was all that he wanted.

But Claudine did not think of that. All her doubts and fears were swept away in the delight of feeling loved and loving – for suddenly she knew she did love Gabry and could not help it, however untrustworthy he might be. And as he was very gentle and tender with her, all the tales about his past loves faded out of her mind for the time being.

She hardly knew how long it was that they were standing there on the stairs, she was quite lost in the discoveries of love, but presently the sound of a door shutting somewhere roused Gabriel to say, "My dearest angel, this is not at all what we ought to be doing. Suppose your aunt were to come out now?"

"Thierry is still playing Mozart," murmured Claudine, with her arm still round his neck.

"But it's a different sonata!" said Gabriel amused. "I must make my apologies to your aunt, Claudine chérie. Would it be better if I went into the drawing room without you?"

Claudine pulled herself together. "Yes, I'll go up to my room and come down again when I've brushed my hair," she said, in matter-of-fact tones which made Gabriel smile again.

They went up to the head of the stairs. Gabriel took off his greatcoat and flung it carelessly over the banister rails. Claudine, who had started up the next flight, looked back at him, suddenly uncertain.

"Come back soon from your Florentine heaven," he said, and kissed her hand as it lay on the polished rail.

Reassured, Claudine ran upstairs and Gabriel walked into the room where Thierry was playing Mozart.

And when Claudine came in, he was comfortably ensconced by the fire, with a cup of coffee, listening to Madame de Lamerle's grumbles about French officialdom. The rest of the evening went by for Claudine in a happy dream; she was still under the spell of the first realisation of love and quite unable to think of all the difficulties and dangers which must lie ahead.

CHAPTER
FOURTEEN

THE evening of the ball came at last and the girls, in their new white dresses of muslin, high-waisted and low-necked, with white stockings and shoes and gloves, were ready long before their aunt. In the two intervening days Gabry had been to the house several times but Claudine had not seen him alone. But even when other people were there, when Laurent was teasing him to talk of the campaigns he had fought in, she felt they were in touch, in sympathy, that he was thinking of her all the time as she was of him, and this made her happy.

Yesterday he had said, when Madame de Lamerle had been out of the room, "I shall be coming to that ball."

"But should you?" Claudine had said anxiously. "Surely it would be dangerous for you to appear at such a public occasion?"

But Gabry had laughed at the idea of its being dangerous. "None of the French here know me," he had said.

All the same, when they walked into the ballroom and Claudine saw how many French officers were present, she trembled inwardly. She was afraid for Gabry; at the same time she could not help feeling that for her the ball would be meaningless without him.

The rooms were well lit and the assembly was well attended; war or no war, people liked to enjoy themselves while they could, and no fighting was going on anywhere near Trier.

Gabriel arrived when the rooms were already full and the ball had begun. Claudine and Seraphine were dancing with two young men belonging to families they had visited with their aunt, while she sat chatting with the mothers and watching.

Claudine noticed at once when Gabry came in, even though he entered behind a group of young men wearing tricolour rosettes to show their republican sympathies. Claudine was amused to see that he too was wearing one. But she could not help feeling that his upright carriage was so soldierly that people would wonder why he was not in uniform.

As soon as they went back to their aunt he came over and bowed to her, asking if he might have the honour of dancing with her eldest niece.

Aunt Charlotte looked slightly taken aback, but could think of no reason to refuse, and so Claudine found herself walking out to take her place in the set with Gabriel for a partner. It seemed very strange. If there had been no Revolution and no war, this was how she might have met him; though probably not at a public assembly but at a private ball, perhaps at Isenbourg. And they might have met many times before they had reached anything like the degree of intimacy to which they had been led by the extraordinary circumstances of their actual meeting.

Gabriel looked less out of place among the republicans than she had feared. Although he was wearing the best clothes he had brought with him, they had not been chosen for fashion, in order to suit the character he had assumed; some of the young republicans of Trier were better dressed though none, Claudine thought, had anything approaching his ease of manner. But his face, weather-beaten after his months in the woods, and scarred as it was, did not suggest the aristocrat of fancy, in spite of those arrogant hawk-like features. Claudine began to be less afraid and even to enjoy the dancing, though they could talk little and then not with any privacy.

"I suppose I cannot dance all the time with you, Concordia," said Gabriel presently. "But will you give me the pleasure of taking you in to supper?"

He danced once with Seraphine, whose merry face showed that she did not realise there might be a real danger for him in the evening; to her, his presence was a splendid joke. But after that, until he could claim Claudine again, he walked about the room, occasionally speaking to other men, but generally, she could not help noticing, watching her.

Her aunt noticed it too and when Claudine was sitting by her she remarked quietly, "Our friend Monsieur Gabry seems to have taken an admiration for you, Claudine. That is rather unfortunate."

"Why do you think so, Aunt Charlotte?" asked Claudine,

picking up her fan, not merely to cool her face but to hide it a little.

"Because I am sure your father would not consider him a suitable husband for you, my dear," said Madame de Lamerle, with a quick sigh. "I must say that you looked very well together. I could not help thinking so, however sternly I must watch that young man."

Claudine smiled at her, pleased. Her eyes went back to Gabriel and she saw, to her alarm, that a French officer was talking to him – a Colonel, she thought, someone in an authoritative position. But almost at once, Gabry saw she was sitting down and came over towards them. The French officer merely smiled and walked off.

"What was that Colonel saying to you?" Claudine asked, as Gabry sat down beside her.

"He thought a fine healthy republican like me ought to be in the French army," said Gabriel, with his twisted smile. "He could see I was a bit older than the young fellows they want to conscript, but he held it out as an inducement that in the republican army I could soon rise to a command, since low birth was no longer a disadvantage."

Claudine could not help laughing. "Oh! But how did you put him off?"

"I made out I was much attracted by the prospect," said Gabry, "but I said I was too much in love with my girl to leave Trèves at present – he quite understood. I hope your aunt is not listening."

In fact Madame de Lamerle was at that moment lecturing Seraphine for laughing too much, as he had noticed before he spoke.

Dancing before supper Claudine had almost forgotten her fears and felt all the delight of going down the set with her chosen partner; the pattern of meeting and parting and meeting again suiting so well with the feelings of courtship that it somehow expressed them.

But when they were at table she grew nervous again, for there were some young republicans and French officers opposite them who appeared already to have had too much to drink and were showing off to giggling girls, toasting the Revolution, Liberty, Equality and anything else they could think of, and calling on everyone near to join in, on pain of being considered traitors to the cause.

"You, Citoyen," one said suddenly to Gabriel, "you have not joined us in drinking glory to the Republic."

"I, Citoyen, have to make the most of my chances while Mademoiselle is not under the eye of her aunt," said Gabriel, for Madame de Lamerle was sitting at another table. He took up Claudine's hand from her lap and kissed it.

The young French officer laughed, complimented Claudine on her beauty, but still called on the stranger to drink with them. And one of the men of Trier said, "I have not seen you here before, Citoyen. Where do you come from?"

"Strasbourg," said Gabry at once, "where we are more devoted to liberty than I think you have been in Trèves. And certainly I will drink with you to Liberty."

So he joined in the toast, and Claudine shyly sipped her wine too, and trembled, wishing these loud-voiced young men were not there. They reminded her too much of Gaston Ferrand and the unfortunate Jules Desroux.

Gabriel had apparently allayed their suspicions but their half-drunken behaviour so annoyed him that he took Claudine away to another table, where a company of older citizens of Trier sat with their daughters firmly under observation and only approved young men present. Gabriel called a waiter to bring Claudine a new dish and whispered to her that he would complain to the master of ceremonies, if it were not for calling attention to himself.

The people at the table all took a good look at them but then continued eating and talking in German. Gabry turned to Claudine and said in elegant French, "And now, mademoiselle, tell me which is your favourite flower?"

Claudine was so amused at this formal sentiment, so reminiscent of the schoolgirls' albums and so unlike the Gabry she knew, that she began to laugh. Then, realising that it was for the benefit of the observers, she replied, "My favourites change with the season. Just now it is snowdrops, because I'm on the lookout for them. I know just where they grow, in the woods at Hautefontaine."

"Hautefontaine!" said Gabriel. "You love that place, don't you?" He looked suddenly pensive. "You don't want to leave it."

"I could leave it, under certain circumstances," said Claudine quietly.

He shot her a look of quick understanding and pleasure but he only said, *"Bien!"* and offered her a dish of sweet-meats.

Claudine thought one of the men at the other end of the table, who look like some kind of minor official, was staring a lot at Gabriel. Presently she whispered, "Do you know that man? The one with ginger eyebrows?"

"Not to my knowledge," said Gabry. "But it's possible he may be wondering if this scarred visage does not remind him of a silly young count whom he may have seen about in Trèves seven years ago. I was here a good deal then, as I think you know."

Reminded of the Marquise, Claudine forgot the official who, indeed, soon addressed himself again to his plate. After a moment she said, "Thierry told me a little more about your first marriage, Gabry. I did not understand before."

"It's useless to pretend I did not behave very badly then," he said seriously. "But perhaps you can realise the situation would be very different now, if you would consent to marry me – I hardly dare say it, in case you fly off in a passion against me again."

"But you know I feel differently now," said Claudine reproachfully.

"So I hoped," said Gabriel, "but this is no place to discuss our affairs. Your aunt is keeping an eye on us, like a good chaperone."

"She does not think my father would approve of you," said Claudine.

Gabry smiled. "I fancy she is right there!" he said. "Listen, is that the music beginning again? Some people are moving. Let us go back to the ballroom before you are made to dance with Franz or Wilhelm or Nicolas."

They did go back, among the first couples, but after that dance Aunt Charlotte gathered Claudine firmly to her side.

"Monsieur Gabry, you must not claim any more dances from my niece," she said sternly to him, though her smile was kindly. Claudine could tell that she liked Gabriel and would have allowed him more favour if she had thought it right.

"What, none at all? Not even the last?" he said, standing before them, very tall, and in spite of the scar, very charming.

Madame de Lamerle shook her head. "We shall not stay till the last," she said, provoking cries of lamentation from Seraphine, who had succeeded in dancing every dance and insisted that she was not in the least tired.

But Claudine, if she could dance no more with Gabriel, was content to go home before the end. He stayed till they went, mostly sitting by Madame de Lamerle and talking to her, and came out to hand them into the Judge's carriage.

As they rattled over the cobbles Claudine watched him walking away through the dark streets, with his high collar up, for there was a cold wind blowing. She felt a sensation of relief that the evening had passed off safely – no one had recognised him.

The next day Monsieur de Trévires arrived. He had come to see his brother-in-law, Xavier de Lamerle, but had been unable to bring his wife as she was confined to her bed with a severe cold. She was rarely ill and it annoyed her not to be able to come, but it was at present impossible. She had sent her husband with strict instructions that he must take charge of Xavier and allow her nephew, Thierry de Ravanger, to continue his journey out of the country.

When she heard this Claudine was in a double alarm – that Gabriel might have to leave at once and that her father would not consent to a hurried marriage, or perhaps any marriage. And now, though she had as many reasons as before for not marrying Gabry, Claudine was too much in love to think so much of them as she had. Besides, she felt she could forgive him his affair with the Marquise, knowing now what a loveless marriage had been forced on him. It was a long time ago, and the lady was now married to someone else, safely far away in England.

But she was sharply reminded of other considerations when, on going with her father to see her uncle Xavier just after dinner, they came upon Gabry sitting in Frau Müller's front parlour with Paulette on his knee, showing her a picture-book. This unexpected sight of Gabriel in a paternal rôle might have held a certain charm for Claudine, had it not suggested that paternity might well account for it; she suddenly remembered the fair woman upstairs.

Monsieur de Trévires was not pleased to see Gabriel d'Erlen.

"I wonder you dare to remain in this country, monsieur," he said. "We expected you to have gone long since."

Gabriel said he was waiting for his cousin, and when he heard that Monsieur de Trévires had come to set Thierry free to leave, he did not look as happy as he should have done.

Paulette had slipped off his knee as he rose to greet the visitors and stood there near him, clutching her book, watching them all with bright dark eyes.

"Paulette, *chérie*, run up to your maman," said Gabry, patting her curly dark head.

He went with them to the back room, where Thierry was sitting with Xavier, reading his office with him. The priest knew most of the Latin psalms by heart, which he had repeated daily for so much of his life. Today he was sitting in his chair in a dressing gown, but he looked extremely fragile. The little room seemed so full that Claudine soon slipped out of it and went back to the parlour.

Frau Müller was in there, clearing on to a tray the remains of the dinner she had served for Thierry and Gabry. She began to talk about them to Claudine, in a friendly way, speaking in the local German, and presently asked her if she did not think Monsieur Gabry much disfigured by his scar.

"But I have never seen him without it," said Claudine.

She was already so used to that scar she hardly noticed it.

"You were a child when it happened, I suppose," said Frau Müller. "But I saw a lot of him before that – he used to lodge here when he came to Trier to see his *émigré* friends."

She gave Claudine a sudden keen, speculative look.

"The Marquise d'Ivranches, I suppose," Claudine said, and because she did not want to sound as if she had any personal interest in the affair, she sounded in fact rather scornful.

"So you know about that? I wondered if you did," said Frau Müller. "I can see Monsieur Gabry is in love with you now." She smiled. "He always likes the fair ones. She was fair too – fairer than you. Well! Fair and false, some say. I suppose one can't talk of falseness where both the lovers are married to others, but it wasn't as if he neglected her. He came over from Luxembourg all the time, right up to the child's birth – and afterwards. Oh, he gave her presents and every attention – not like some, who lose interest as soon as a woman is with child." Frau Müller slapped the plates on the tray. "That didn't stop her from taking up with one of those French *émigré* nobles, as soon as she was fit to go out again."

Claudine did not want to appear too interested but curiosity constrained her to ask, "What did he do about that?"

"Of course he wasn't going to show that he cared," returned Frau Müller. "But it must have been humiliating, because everyone was laughing that the baby was as like him as it could stare – I know, because I found a wet nurse for it – she was a friend of mine. Funny, I suppose he's quite a little boy now, that baby – he was older than Paulette, a good deal."

Claudine felt a sensation of physical nausea at the mention of Paulette, compounded of jealousy and anger, so strong as to take her by surprise. It was not because of the child but because of the mother, here in this house.

Frau Müller did not notice, absorbed in her own reminiscences. "Monsieur le Comte had the best room upstairs, of course," she said. "I just happened to be cleaning the stairs one day and I heard him talking to a friend – I can follow French talk. The gentleman was saying, 'You will fight him, I suppose?' And Monsieur d'Erlen said, as savage as anything, 'Fight over that trollop? Be damned if I will!' That's what he said, near enough. He spent most of that night drinking in the tavern across the street and that man of his, Norbert, had to half carry him back here, but after that he went home to Luxembourg, never came back here any more."

Claudine had recovered herself during this recital, partly because Gabry's reactions seemed so typical she could almost have laughed, if she had not been so hurt and angry at his present liaison.

"I think it is strange of the Marquise to cast him off like that, if, as you say, he had behaved almost like a husband when the baby was born," she said.

"It's my belief that's just what she didn't like," said Frau Müller. "From things the wet nurse told me, I think Madame found him too possessive and at the same time not willing to spend all his time with her, because he was a soldier like his father. But her new lover was a courtier, content to live an idle life with cards and gossip – he was French too, which she liked. But not so handsome as our Monsieur Gabry in those days. Still, I think he was well rid of her, though I understand it didn't send him back to his wife, bad fellow!" She laughed, suddenly. "No, he's not virtuous! But I like him, always have. I was pleased as anything when I opened the door and saw him there with Mathilde and little Paulette."

"What? What do you mean?" Claudine asked, her heart giving an uncomfortable jump.

"Last year, before he went into Luxembourg, that was," said Frau Müller. "Yes, and I said, 'What, are you with Mathilde now, monsieur?' Because she used to live here too, you see, before she went off to Vienna. And that's where he'd met her again, it seems. And he laughed a lot and said, 'Mathilde is my wife and Paulette is my daughter, please remember it, Frau Hanna!' "

"His wife?" repeated Claudine, with a gasp.

"Oh, not in law, you understand," said Frau Müller. "On his papers. He had to have false papers to come into French territory and so he had Mathilde put in as a wife. He said that suited them both; it was a great joke with them."

It was not a joke Claudine could appreciate. She stood there, still in her bonnet and pelisse, wishing she could escape from the stuffy room, its windows tight shut, the smell of food lingering and the stove warming the enclosed, used air. She gazed at Frau Müller, wondering why she was telling her all this, having started by saying she thought Gabry was now in love with her. If it was meant as a warning, or a deterrent, it was told with surprising relish and humour, as if Claudine would be sure to appreciate every detail.

She was just wondering if she could ask Frau Müller to fetch her father, so that she could go home, when she heard the door down the passage open and shut, and then next moment Gabriel appeared in the doorway.

Whereupon Frau Müller, with a wide grin on her heavy features, making her look like a clown, made haste to depart with her tray. Gabriel held the door for her, smiling, and bowed her off, so that she clattered away with loud laughter.

But when Gabry turned round and saw Claudine's face, his smile vanished.

"What is it, my love? Are you anxious about your uncle? But he seems better today."

He came towards her but Claudine quickly retreated

round the table, which in that cramped room made an effective barrier. She shook her head, but could find no words to say. It was anger, not grief, that made her speechless.

Gabry said, "If it's your father's arrival that has upset you, Claudine, don't you think the best thing is for me to speak to him at once about us? I know he won't like it, but if he would countenance an engagement, at least I could see something of you before I have to go."

"No," said Claudine. She felt as if she were choking. "No. I don't want to do that."

Gabriel looked at her with a slight frown twisting his black brows. "It seems to me dishonourable not to," he said.

"Dishonourable!" cried Claudine. "Honour! What a splendid word for you to use!"

"My dearest girl, what has made you so angry suddenly?" said Gabry, in surprise.

"It seems dishonourable to you not to tell my father you want to marry me," said Claudine, "but not at all dishonourable to make love to two women at once! Well, it does to me! And it shows me just how little you mean with your kissing and kind words."

"But what are you talking about?" said Gabriel, and Claudine thought he was remarkably good at ignoring the obvious. "You are the only person I love – and believe me, I know the difference now between love and the kind of infatuation I once had for Marie-Claire."

"Marie-Claire?" said Claudine, whose mind was full of Mathilde upstairs.

"The Marquise – Milady something-or-other, as she is now," said Gabriel. "I suppose old Frau Hanna has been talking about all that; it was a great drama to her and she enjoyed every minute of it, but it's a long time ago. Claudine! Where's your sense of humour? You can't have been more than eleven when the whole thing was over."

"I am not thinking of her," Claudine said. "I suppose you don't even consider Paulette's mother as worth mentioning, because she is not well born."

"Mathilde!" said Gabriel, in the tone of one who had indeed forgotten the existence of that person. "What has she got to do with it? Oh – she is on my false papers as my wife, of course, but that's only for the benefit of the French. Surely old Frau Hanna hasn't been telling you I've got a secret wife hidden away upstairs? She likes a joke, but that's going a bit far." He started to come round the table. "Claudine, I promise you, there's nothing to prevent us marrying according to all the laws of God and man. Surely you don't think I would suggest applying to your father, if there was some serious impediment?"

Claudine, bewildered by this practical language and his unconcerned tone, backed away from him towards the window. She thought of Mathilde on his arm, smiling up at him, before he knew of her own presence in Trèves; she thought of Frau Müller saying how they had both laughed and said the marriage arrangement suited them both.

"And what do you say to *her*?" she demanded furiously. "Do you say, 'Mademoiselle Claudine is the kind of girl I can marry, and you aren't, but that need not present any impediment?' Do you propose to pension her off when you marry me? Or send her back to Vienna so that she is conveniently there when you get bored with me?"

She said it all in a passion, but in a low voice and nearly in tears, for her own feelings had suddenly become quite unmanageable. She was shocked at what she heard herself saying, but could not stop herself.

"Claudine . . ." said Gabriel, advancing another couple of steps.

But she said fiercely, "Don't come any nearer!" She felt she could not bear any contact at this moment. "I never can believe anything you say! I saw you with her, and Paulette, in the town – you didn't see us. It's no use your denying it. I wish I had never thought I could trust you! But I know you won't understand. Oh, I am so – unhappy!"

She was on the verge of breaking into helpless crying and struggling hard not to succumb, for if he were to try and comfort her, she felt she might weaken towards him.

But at that moment Thierry and her father could be heard in the passage outside and Gabry had only just time to move away from Claudine before they entered the room. Claudine stood with her back to the window, hoping that her face would remain unscrutinised.

Her mother would certainly have noticed that something was amiss but Gautier de Trévires was not sensitive to feelings and atmosphere. Claudine saw Thierry glance from her stiff figure to Gabry's unsmiling and sombre face, but her father only said, "Well, Claudine, ready to go back to Aunt Charlotte's?"

"Certainly, *mon père*."

Her voice sounded a little unsteady to herself, but he did not notice.

"Xavier may last many months, but I am sure he cannot make that long journey, poor fellow," said Monsieur de Trévires. "We shall take care of him, now. When will you leave, Thierry?"

"I shall have to discuss it with Monsieur d'Erlen," said Thierry.

Monsieur de Trévires just acknowledged the existence of Monsieur d'Erlen by the faintest of bows and then, taking his daughter's arm, went out of the house. Gabriel said not a word.

As they walked away Claudine caught a last glimpse of him, standing in the window, looking out after her. He did not look unconcerned now. His expression was moody and bitter. The sight of that dark face, with its hard outline, made her realise how little she really knew him. And yet, when she remembered their kisses on the stairs, and the dancing at the ball, and her happiness for the last few days, she could hardly keep back her tears.

Monsieur de Trévires talked about the Roman remains in Trèves all the way back to the Judge's house.

CHAPTER
FIFTEEN

ONCE she was alone in her bedroom, Claudine could hold back her tears no longer and having begun she could not stop; she gave herself a headache with crying. Aunt Charlotte, who guessed that the imminent departure of the Comte de Villerange might have something to do with her niece's indisposition, told her to go to bed early and sent up a maid to light her fire and bring her some supper. Unlaced and sitting wrapped in her loose bed-gown by the fire, Claudine was startled when one of the older kitchen servants suddenly came into the room. She was a Luxembourger and spoke in the dialect.

"Mademoiselle, I have a message for you," she said, and held out a folded scrap of paper, smiling.

Claudine took it. She was sitting with only a couple of candles in a branched stick but it was easy enough to read the scribbled French words.

"I beg you to let me speak to you. – G."

She looked at the old woman. "Speak to me? What does he mean?"

"Mademoiselle, he's outside in the street, waiting. You could go down to that little room by the door – I'm minding the door while Hans has his supper. Oh! He's very anxious to see you, my dear little mademoiselle!"

"But I can't," said Claudine. "No, no, I can't."

"I could help you into your gown again, mademoiselle," said the woman, evidently, like all the Luxembourg servants, taking Gabriel d'Erlen's side in any difficulty. "He said to me, 'For God's sake, Marie, bring her down. I must see her.'"

"But it is quite impossible," said Claudine.

It was not merely that she was half undressed; she felt sure it would be plain to Gabry that she had been crying and though she was unhappy, she was still angry with him. She thought to herself, "He thinks it will be like that time on the stairs – he will easily win me over."

And so she firmly ordered old Marie to go down and say she was not coming. But after the old woman had left the room, shaking her head and clicking her tongue, Claudine crept to the window, slipped behind the curtains and pulled the shutter open a crack to peep out.

There was a lamp fixed in a bracket by their door and by the light of it she could see Gabriel pacing up and down the street, restless and impatient. It was trying to snow; specks of white were floating in the air. He had a hat on and his collar up round his ears, but he was now an unmistakable figure to her; she knew his way of walking, every characteristic gesture.

Claudine watched old Marie, with a black shawl over her head, trot out into the street and Gabriel turn quickly towards her. It was evidently some time before he could believe Claudine had refused to see him, but at last he gave a coin to the old woman and began to walk away. At the corner of the street he stopped and turned to look up at the house, perhaps to find her window.

Claudine leaned into the corner of the embrasure, pushing the shutter close again with her finger. Her heart was beating hard. When, presently, she dared to peep again, he was gone.

She did not tell Seraphine when her sister came to bed, but Seraphine saw she had been crying, and with sympathy and curiosity soon elicited that Gabriel d'Erlen was the cause.

"I believe you are in love with him, Claudine," she said.

"Much good it would do me, if I were," Claudine said bitterly.

"But he seems to be so much in love with you," said Seraphine. "When we were dancing, at the ball, he asked me if you had had any suitors *before* – as if he were one now. Perhaps he did mean it, Claudine, when he asked you to marry him."

"I daresay," answered Claudine, as resolutely as she could, "but I don't intend to marry a man I can't trust. Please don't talk about it any more, Seraphine. He must go soon and I want to try to forget all about it."

Seraphine looked doubtful, but recently she had found her sister hard to understand. Claudine, usually so calm and dreamy, had suddenly become unpredictable; for a few days smiling and singing and now suddenly resentful and desolate. "If that's what love does to people it can't be such fun as one supposes," Seraphine said to herself, as they got into bed and let down the curtains.

The next day Claudine found that her aunt had invited Thierry and Gabriel to dinner. She wondered whether Gabry would find some excuse to stay away, but he came, rather to her embarrassment, though he was silent, and after the first greeting hardly seemed to notice her.

Monsieur de Trévires was in an argumentative mood; he started talking politics with Thierry at dinner, and in spite of Madame de Lamerle's efforts, insisted on continuing in the drawing room, when they were taking coffee. He several times tried to include Gabriel in the conversation but he refused to be drawn. But at last Monsieur de Trévires, who had been eloquently discoursing on the principles of republicanism, directly demanded his opinion.

"Monsieur, I fear it will not be to your liking," said Gabry.

Gautier de Trévires smiled. "Well, I do not expect agreement from you, Monsieur de Villerange! But I hope I am able to accept a reasonable disagreement."

"I am not a theoretician like you, monsieur," said Gabry. "I daresay the present rulers of France can defend their principles, but I do not think much of their practice. And as far as Luxembourg is concerned I regard them as enemies and I shall continue to fight them until they are driven out or I am killed."

Claudine thought her father had expected some political argument, not a simple declaration of intent. He looked somewhat put out, but then began to argue that a republican government might do more for the people of Luxembourg than the old system. She had often heard his views before and indeed had accepted them herself, though she had always been sorry for the peasants who rebelled.

Thierry had been arguing that it was possible to introduce reforms into the old régime, which in any case had been less unjust in their country than in France. Gabry was plainly not much interested in theory. But his straightforward statement of his own conviction had impressed Claudine, even against her will. After all, there was no necessity for his risking his life by coming back to his occupied country and throwing in his lot with the rebels, in an attempt, hopeless as it had turned out, to rid Luxembourg of a foreign yoke.

Claudine felt uncomfortably ashamed to have been thinking so much about herself; had she not been to him simply a distraction, complicating his task, rather than giving him support? It was all very well for her to take a high line about love, but was not her own very selfish?

She was as silent as he all the evening, and was glad when her aunt, to break up the political argument, asked Thierry to play for them, for her silence was then unremarkable. She was even able to sing, when her father requested it of her. She did not sing the ballad she had sung to the echo, but another old song, celebrating the woods and hills of their country, the rivers and the nymphs supposedly haunting their depths.

Claudine had a sweet clear voice and she sang simply, with no affectations. In the fading afternoon light, in the winter town, there was something enchanting in the young voice singing of the country whose fate they had just been arguing over – the country itself, the loved place.

Charlotte de Lamerle thought of Constant, her husband, dying in defence of his home at Solveringen, and was glad the room had gone shadowy.

Almost as soon as this song was ended Gabry suddenly took his leave, rather to their surprise, for Thierry was staying on. He made some confused excuse and hurried away; as he said goodbye to her, Claudine had an impression of strong feeling suppressed. She did not dare to look at him and her farewell was almost inaudible.

Claudine was already beginning to regret her outburst, and next morning she was glad to be called down to the drawing room to see Thierry; she hoped to talk about Gabry to him. But she was not prepared to see the person he had brought with him, none other than the fair Mathilde, mother of Paulette. There was no one else in the room.

Claudine stopped on the threshold.

"Come in, *chère cousine*," said Thierry, limping to meet her. "I have brought Madame Mathilde to meet you. She wants to speak privately to you, so if you go and sit in the window over there, I will stay here and play."

He sat down on the pianoforte, and began some variations of Mozart's which Claudine had often heard before.

As the two women walked up to the room together,

Claudine was overcome with a mixture of shyness and curiosity. Mathilde was a mature woman of thirty; she was not at all vulgar or brazen but seemed almost as shy as Claudine herself.

"Mademoiselle," she said, as they sat down, "you will think me very bold in seeking this interview. It is Monsieur de Ravanger who suggested it. He had some conversation with his cousin last night which convinced him that – that you are under a misapprehension about me."

Claudine was much too embarrassed to speak. Now that she was sitting opposite this woman she wished more than ever that she had not voiced her suspicions to Gabriel.

Mathilde went on, after a moment, "It is true that Monsieur Gabry brought me back to Trier, and got false papers in which I was written as the wife of Paul Gabry – we chose the name of Paul because of Paulette. He said it was a good disguise for him to travel with a wife and child, but I think he really did it to help me to get home. We met again in Vienna, mademoiselle, something over a year ago, when I was in great straits."

"Again?" said Claudine.

Mathilde nodded. "I knew him here, before. I think you know he was in Trier often when a certain lady was living here. At that time I was living with a man who was not married to me, a French *émigré* who knew Monsieur d'Erlen. He was always telling me we should marry, but after I had gone with him to Vienna, and had my little Paulette, he deserted me to marry a rich Austrian widow – she lived a long way off in another town, I never discovered where. He gave me money at first, but then it stopped coming, and I was very hard pressed. I did sewing, but it was a struggle, and I longed to come home. My family are respectable vintners up the Moselle, but they cast me off when they found how I was living. Mademoiselle, I don't defend my conduct, but I was well paid for my folly, I assure you. Just when I thought we should starve, I met Monsieur d'Erlen, and he was so kind, and took us out to dinner. He was angry because Austria had made peace with France. 'I am going back to Luxembourg,' he said, 'to see if we can't cause those French devils some trouble.' And when he heard how much I wanted to get back to Trier, he had this idea of bringing me as his wife. You know how high-spirited he is   he made a great joke of it, especially to Frau Müller – but I hope you do not think . . . I hope no one imagines that there was any other association between us.

"I did not half-starve myself as a sempstress in Vienna, in order to come home with a reputation for bad living. As for Monsieur le Comte, he says that when he has gone away, I must pretend to hear of his death, and when I am safely a widow, I may perhaps find a respectable husband. That's what he says, and when he came back from Luxembourg a few weeks ago, he was full of jokes, pointing out men we passed in the town and saying, 'How would he do? Too fat? But fatness shows a fat purse, Mathilde!' " She smiled at Claudine.

It was impossible to disbelieve her, impossible not to recognise Gabry's style in the remarks she attributed to him. Claudine felt overcome with shame.

"I am very sorry," she stammered, feeling hot all over. "Somehow, what Frau Müller said seemed . . . it was inexcusable of me."

"On the contrary, mademoiselle, it was very natural," said Mathilde kindly. "We know that Monsieur le Comte has not a very good reputation in this respect! But I must tell you that I do not think he is the sort of man to whom women are nothing but a casual pleasure. His love affairs may have been wrong, but they were not heartless – nor do I think there have been many since he went back to fight in your country. You see, I defend him; that is because he had been kind to me, and it would be a poor return for his kindness to allow you to think him as bad as he is made out to be. People always like to make the worst of the sins of others! I know, for having once done wrong, one is taken to be altogether shameless. I expect it is hard for you, so very young, and so well guarded by your good family, to understand these differences. But do you believe me, about Monsieur le Comte?"

Claudine looked into her good-natured blue eyes and knew that she did. "It is very good of you to tell me this," she said at last. "I have had some very unjust thoughts about you; it makes me ashamed."

Mathilde smiled. "It is the thoughts about him which I hope to correct," she said. "For his cousin has told me that he is very much in love with you, and nearly in despair that you should now refuse to speak to him. And if I were you, mademoiselle, I should try to forgive him what is past. After all, he is a man over thirty; it would be most surprising if he had not had some affairs of the heart before this. But I know they have not brought him much happiness – so there is your chance, if you love him. For if you make him happy, I do not think he will make you unhappy. Excuse me, if I am taking a liberty in speaking to you what I think, straight out."

Claudine made her understand that she was not offended but grateful. Indeed, Mathilde's story, while it made her fee she could hardly dare to look Gabry in the face again, lifted a great weight off her heart – the suspicion that he was nothing but a philanderer, fickle and shallow, a mere pleasure-seeker in love. She did not need to be adjured to forgive Gabry's past; that had only worried her as reflected in the present. She felt disposed to trust the wisdom of a woman like Mathilde, who had learned by experience, and had survived disillusion without becoming embittered against all men, like old Victoire at Villerange.

They rose and walked down the room; Thierry ended his playing with some triumphant chords and a wide smile, guessing from Claudine's face that Mathilde's confession had produced the effect he had hoped.

"Mind, Gabry knows nothing of this," he said. "I suggested to him that he should tell me to tell you the truth but he did not think it fair to Mathilde to tell her story. I knew she would feel as I did, so I addressed myself to her." He smiled at Mathilde.

Claudine could not help wondering, in that case, what Gabry had proposed to tell her when he sent her his scribbled message – perhaps he would have just sworn there was nothing in it. Would she have believed him? Claudine was afraid not.

"Thierry," she said, "I ought to see him myself now."

Her cousin immediately suggested that she should walk back with them, and since Madame de Lamerle and Seraphine had gone to watch Laurent's fencing lesson, Claudine agreed and hurried away to put on her warm pelisse and fur bonnet, for it was still very cold and there was snow on the ground.

But when they reached the lodging house they found Gabriel was not there. Claudine went to greet her uncle, who said he was delighted to be interrupted from reading the newspaper, since there seemed to be nothing in it but disaster and misery.

"The sight of your dear young face is quite a refreshment," he said.

Claudine sat with him till a priest came to see him. This, once so ordinary an event, now seemed to Xavier de Lamerle a special providence. He had not been able to see another priest since his imprisonment and, being well aware of his serious condition, was anxious to make his confession. The priest who came looked like some shabby clerk, for he was wearing secular clothes; like Xavier himself he had refused the oath and was in hiding.

Claudine left them together and went into the small front parlour carrying her pelisse on her arm. She put it over an upright chair and then sat down on the small hard couch by the stove. Thierry had disappeared upstairs and she now had time to wonder how she was going to face Gabriel, after what she had said to him and what she had learned since. After a few minutes it seemed so impossible that she was ready to get up and flee, but before she had made a move, she heard someone stamping snow off his boots on the doorstep and the next moment Gabriel walked into the room, carrying a long loaf of bread under his arm.

Directly he saw her he stopped and stood still.

Then he said, with stiff formality, "If you do not wish to see me, mademoiselle, I will withdraw at once."

This was dreadful. "But I do want to see you, Gabry," Claudine replied nervously. "That's why I came here."

He seemed so tall and remote, standing above her, that she wished she could get up and speak to him face to face; but her knees felt too weak and she could not move.

"So! . . . But why do you come now, when you refused before to see me?" he demanded, less coldly, but with some bitterness.

He put the bread on the table and threw his hat beside it, but he did not sit down. He stood there looking down at her and she dropped her gaze. How was she ever going to say what she must say?

"I could not go down that night – I had retired," she whispered. "And besides, I did not then know the truth about Mathilde. I do now. She has told me herself."

"Mathilde has told you?" he said, in surprise. "But how

could she know anything about it? Of course I could not
speak of it to her."

"It was Thierry," said Claudine. "He told her." She managed to look up at last and to say anxiously, "I am sorry
indeed that I spoke as I did. At the time, it was such a shock
to me, Gabry, I hardly knew what I was saying. I have been
very much ashamed since."

Gabriel was gazing at her, as if he could hardly take in her
words.

"So, you believe Mathilde?" he said at last. "But you did
not believe me."

Claudine began to realise how deeply her angry words
about his untrustworthiness had sunk into his mind.

"But I have never deceived you in anything, Claudine," he
said. "Unless in not telling you at once that I was Erlen of
Villerange. I haven't even tried to hide my bad character –
not that I could have done so there, where everyone knows all
about me. But I suppose that is why you think I am capable of
any kind of infidelity and betrayal."

"I don't think it now, Gabry," said Claudine earnestly.
"Horrible as this has been, it has taught me much about
myself and I think something about you, too. I didn't know
how nasty I could be – so jealous and hateful."

"Jealous?" said Gabry, surprised.

Suddenly, to her great relief, he sat down on the couch
beside her.

"Yes, terribly," she said, and smiled at him. "I don't mind
about the past, but I found I couldn't bear the idea of your
loving someone else in the present. It seemed to turn it all
into something so trivial. And to me, it isn't, you see. To me
it is like – I don't know – discovering the meaning of life . . .
as important as that." And then she added, "I expect you
think that is silly and sentimental."

He was looking at her intently, but although sitting so
near, not touching her. She saw a look of trouble in his eyes.

"What is the matter, Gabry?" she asked gently, at last.
"Don't you think I am sorry enough for all those horrible
things I said? But I wish you could forget them now."

"Claudine, it's not that at all," he said with an effort. "It's
because I know very well I've no right to expect you to believe
in me, still less to love me. And though I can't imagine the
state of mind of anyone who could spend half his time with

Mathilde and the other half protesting love to you, yet I have to admit that after Marie-Claire threw me over I did try to get what I could out of associations with other women which I knew in my heart were just what you called them – trivial. All I can say is that this last year in Luxembourg gave me something better to do than pursue other men's faithless wives. But I know that does not make me any more fit to love someone like you. The more generous you are, the more conscious I am that you deserve somebody altogether better than I am. At the same time, after the misery of the last two days, I can't bear to think of losing you. So you see how selfish I am."

Claudine shyly put her hand on his. It was the first time she had made an advance to him.

"But I can't do without you, either," she said quietly.

She was pleased when she saw the teasing gleam come back into his hazel-green eyes, so near to hers that she could detect every change of feeling.

"Dear blessed Child of Nature!" he said. "So! I have something to thank that tiresome genius Monsieur Rousseau for – your frank honesty!"

He kissed her hand and held it close in both his as he said, "Do you mean that you will risk it after all, and marry me?"

Claudine smiled at him. "Yes, monsieur."

"And it won't be 'No! I hate you!' tomorrow?" he said.

"I only hated you because I loved you," Claudine said seriously.

It made Gabry laugh, though he said, in the midst of his laugheter, "I know what you mean, Concordia." He put his arm round her then broke out, "Confound this greatcoat! I might as well be in armour."

He got up to pull it off and Claudine remarked, "Seraphine would say you looked even more like the Thirty Years' War Count, at Villerange."

"Oh, would she?" said Gabry, flinging the coat over the end of the couch. It slipped off on to the floor, but he let it lie. "That old villain? I can see I am going to have trouble with that little sister-in-law!"

He sat down again and said to her, "There are all sorts of difficulties, before us, my dear angel, but I'm not going to worry about them just yet. I want to make sure first about that hate of yours really being love."

Claudine was more than willing that he should. Since that time on the stairs at the Judge's house an age seemed to have gone by and her own feelings to have changed so much it was as if she had become years older in the interval. She felt she knew Gabry much better too, his real as opposed to his reported character, and why he set so much store on her love, because he had never found it with those women she had once been so jealous of. The vague romantic feeling that had made the ball seem like an exciting dream had become something much more definite and personal, and more real too.

They sat on Frau Müller's uncomfortable sofa and forgot everything but each other, the time as well, and so were taken completely by surprise when the door opened and in walked Monsieur de Trévires.

When he saw his daughter leaning back on the couch, lovingly entwined with that undesirable representative of a corrupt aristocracy, the Comte de Villerange, Gautier de Trévires was, for once in his unemotional life, shocked into furious anger.

"Claudine!"

There was such a degree of parental horror in his voice that Claudine jumped to her feet – and then wished she had not, because it must seem like guilt. Gabriel certainly got up more slowly.

"Monsieur d'Erlen, you have well repaid me for shielding you from the French authorities," Gautier de Trévires said bitterly, "by corrupting my daughter. I would not have thought even you would do so base a thing."

"Monsieur de Trévires, do not insult your daughter," Gabriel returned stiffly. "She has promised to marry me."

"Marry?" Gautier de Trévires said sarcastically. "And why have I not been informed, in that case? Marriage! My poor Claudine, is this how he has persuaded you to behave with such abandon?"

"We were going to speak to you, Papa, please believe it," said Claudine.

"I daresay you believe it," her father answered sharply. "But I know very well that my daughter would not be considered a match for an Erlen of Villerange, even if my principles did not put me in opposition to all that family stands for. No, it is clear to me how he has deceived you with promises of marriage which he is not in a position to fulfil – and I only hope I have discovered this affair before it has gone further than kisses."

Claudine, who was standing close to Gabry, felt him go tense with anger at this accusation and she was afraid he would be carried away by one of his sudden bursts of rage, as he had been with his cousin Thierry. She thought he was going to strike her father in the face, and he was so much taller and stronger that it was her father she feared for. In spite of this, her recent experience had made her realise that Gabry was extremely vulnerable where she was concerned; he must not think she took her father's side against him.

And so it was to him she turned, grasping his arms.

"Gabry, don't be angry," she said quickly. "Do remember that Papa knows nothing of all that has passed between us before this. We have taken him by surprise. Let me explain it to him."

Gabriel was silent for a moment, but she could tell that the danger of a blind surge of anger was past. Not so his fears about her, however.

"If you go with him now, he will never allow you to see me again," he said, with a kind of passionate despair which surprised her.

"You are entirely right in that supposition, monsieur," Gautier de Trévires said coldly.

"I promise you, Gabry, I will not give you up," Claudine assured him earnestly. "I am going to marry you, but I have a duty to my father too."

"He will persuade you against me," said Gabriel, with gloomy conviction.

Claudine saw that he did not have complete confidence in her love; not because he thought her faithless but because, aware of his own past and of her youth, he feared that she would not be able to persevere against parental disapproval.

But he said to her father, "Monsieur de Trévires, I understand your fears very well. However, in spite of appearances, which I admit are against me, I did not intend to carry off Claudine without applying for your permission. I would like to assure you now that once we are across the Rhine I am well able to give her a proper establishment. I ask you to refer to Monsieur de Ravanger, if you doubt that my intentions are honourable."

Monsieur de Trévires, if not shaken by this formal speech

from his daughter's seducer, was at any rate restored to his customary cool manner. He bowed stiffly and held out his hand to Claudine.

Anxious to give Gabry a final reassurance of her love, and unable to do it with a kiss because he was too tall, Claudine put his hand against her face before she let it go, and then went to her father.

If she had not been so full of anxious feelings, she might have noticed the look of disapproval, not to say distaste, with which Monsieur de Trévires regarded this loving gesture. His pale face seemed to shrink even closer to the bones, but he said nothing. He picked up her pelisse, determined that he and not Gabry should help her into it, and then, without another word, took her arm and marched her out of the house.

CHAPTER
SIXTEEN

NEVER had Monsieur de Trévires wished so keenly for the presence of his wife as now in dealing with his elder daughter. He had always thought of Claudine as more his child than hers; she had listened to him, taken her ideas from him, read the books he recommended and discussed them intelligently with him, walking in the woods at Hautefontaine or sitting in the library while the rain beat down outside. She had fired at the great ideals of liberty and justice which he had set before her, ready to believe that when men threw off the yoke of the monarchs they would govern themselves like a band of brothers. Since the year of the Terror Monsieur de Trévires himself had entertained serious doubts of this, though he was inclined to think that Parisians were not representative of mankind in general.

But now here was his beautiful Claudine looking at him with her wide gentle grey eyes, and instead of being the lovely echo of all his ideals, she was quietly persistent in her determination to marry someone not merely of the opposite persuasion but, Gautier de Trévires felt, a man without any ideals of all, who fought as his ancestors had fought, in defence of his own order and his own possessions.

Claudine might maintain that Gabriel d'Erlen had been fighting for the peasants of Luxembourg, but her father thought otherwise.

"Nonsense, my dear; he came as a spy for the Austrians and fought because he is a man who cannot keep out of a fight."

"Well, his men are devoted to him," said Claudine. "And what are they but the People you talk so much about, Papa?"

"They are misled as to their true interests," he maintained.

There was a slight pause and then Claudine said, "I am sure Gabry would not oppress people, and if I were his wife, I could help him to do more for them."

"You are assuming that the Austrians will drive the French out of our country," said Monsieur de Trévires, pacing the room.

"Yes," said Claudine. "After all, we are more German than French – look at our language."

Monsieur de Trévires, resisting the temptation to argue the point of history, returned to the subject of Gabriel d'Erlen.

"In any case, Claudine, how can you think of uniting yourself for life to a man like that?" he said. "I hardly like to tell you the way in which he has lived, but it is not such as to give me any hopes of your permanent happiness."

"I know all about that," his daughter returned calmly. "It did worry me at first because I thought he had just taken a fancy to me and all the talk of marrying was because he thought I was the kind of girl who would not yield to him otherwise."

Monsieur de Trévires stopped still and stared at her. At last he said, "And pray, what made you change your mind, Claudine?"

"Knowing him better," said Claudine.

Then she told her father something, suitably edited, of her acquaintance with Gabriel, and his proposal at Christmas, which she had refused.

"A proposal at Christmas! Why did you not inform me? Or your mother?"

"I did not expect to see him again," said Claudine. "I wanted to forget him as soon as I could." She smiled suddenly. "I couldn't all the same, even then."

Monsieur de Trévires stared at her with suspicions confirmed.

"The truth is, you are infatuated with the fellow," he said. "I grant you he is well-made enough and has the air and manner to charm a woman. But, my dear child, I thought you would have more sense than to be carried away by that sort of thing."

"Papa, it is no good your trying to make me despise Gabriel," said Claudine. "I really love him. I don't think he's perfect, but neither am I. Perhaps we shall quarrel sometimes; I don't care. I am happy with him. He's not a complicated person, like you – I expect that's why you can't understand him. But that's what I like: his directness."

"Direct!" said Monsieur de Trévires with a snort. "Headstrong! Used to getting his own way!"

"Headstrong, I daresay," said Claudine, "but as for getting his own way, he has not done so. What with his father, his forced marriage, and the war, he has been a good deal thwarted. And I do admit that a Gabry who *had* always had his own way could easily be intolerable!" She laughed, and her father was again amazed at her determination and the ease with which she spoke of her lover and defended him to the person who till now had always been for her the first authority.

"I wish your mother were here," he said, temporarily defeated.

"Maman, I know, does not approve Monsieur d'Erlen's reputation," said Claudine, "though she might understand him if she knew him better. But don't you think, Papa, that she would not be unwilling to see me the Comtesse de Villerange?"

Gautier de Trévires knew as well as she did that this would indeed weigh very strongly with Madame his wife. There was a silence.

Then he took out his watch. "Good heavens! I must go. I have to be at the French headquarters in half an hour, to discuss something of importance. Now, Claudine, promise me that if Monsieur d'Erlen should call, you will not see him alone."

"Certainly, Papa," said Claudine dutifully, rising and curtsying. "I will tell him to come back later when you are at home."

Monsieur de Trévires decided that to say anything more would signal his defeat, so he kissed his daughter and departed forthwith.

Claudine sat down, smiling to herself, alone in the drawing-room. She thought she would bring him round in the end.

A few minutes later Seraphine and Laurent came in, bursting with curiosity.

It was afternoon; they had all had dinner and during that meal the younger ones had guessed that something was going on between Claudine and her father, even before they were closeted together in the drawing room. Madame de Lamerle had gone out with her brother the Judge to dine with friends and they were not expected back till late.

Claudine had now no objection to talking about her proposed marriage, and so Seraphine's curiosity was satisfied at last. Laurent, who had conceived a great admiration for Gabriel d'Erlen, was delighted at the prospect.

"Oh, I shall almost be his cousin!" he cried.

Claudine could see that Seraphine was pondering her recent rapid changes of front and signalled with her eyes not to pursue inquiry in front of Laurent. Even to her sister, some things were going to be hard to explain.

Luckily there were other questions on which Seraphine's curiosity was equally intense. "What does Papa say?" was one and "When will you be married, and where?" another.

When and where she could be married to someone who was at present living under a false name and in hiding from the French was something of which Claudine had as yet hardly dared to think. But she could relate Papa's views and they were still discussing them when Ernest Pelt appeared at the door.

"Mademoiselle Claudine, there's a young man below who says he is your father's secretary. He's come straight from Luxembourg and says if your father is out he must see you, for he has very urgent news. He says his name is Lefèvre."

"Rémy!" said Seraphine. "Bring him up, Ernest."

Rémy came upstairs with a hurried yet dragging step which told of someone too tired to go as fast as he wished, and when they saw him his weariness was evident in his anxious face. Claudine sent Ernest for wine and made Rémy sit down by the stove, but he could hardly sit still, tired though he was.

"Mademoiselle Claudine, Monsieur Thierry is in great danger," he said. "Where is he? I must go and warn him at once."

"I can direct you – I can take you there," said Claudine. "But Rémy, you look ready to faint. Why is Cousin Thierry in danger?"

"It is all because of Monsieur d'Erlen," said Rémy, with the old resentment in his voice. "Listen, you may not know it, but he is still here, in Trier."

Laurent began to laugh. "Oh! We do know it!" he said.

Rémy stared at him but went on, "I was in Luxembourg recently and just happened to be with some of the garrison officers when a man arrived from Trier – a civilian. He was a

Luxembourger who had gone there on business and was invited to a public ball. He saw Monsieur d'Erlen and recognised him. What a stupid thing to do, to go to a ball! So as to meet some woman, I suppose."

Claudine suddenly remembered the man who had stared at Gabry when they had moved from the table with the drunken young men. "This informer – had he gingery eyebrows and a red face?"

Rémy looked at her with sudden suspicion. "Yes."

"But even if he recognised Monsieur d'Erlen, how did he know about Thierry?" Seraphine wanted to know.

"Because he followed Monsieur d'Erlen back to his lodging and saw there were other Luxembourgers there," said Rémy. "He didn't know Monsieur Thierry was the Comte d'Isenbourg, but he's guessed he was the lame notary who got that priest away before Christmas. He was up in all the cases because he's been acting as clerk with the police. It's bad luck he came to Trier, but if Monsieur d'Erlen hadn't been such a fool as to attend a public ball, he would never have known either of them was here." He got to his feet, just as Ernest came back with the wine. "I can't sit here, and let them take Monsieur Thierry by surprise. They may be in Trier already. My horse cast a shoe, and I was delayed."

"They?" Claudine said. "Who? Who may be here?"

"Captain Ferrand and a whole bunch of men," said Rémy, "of course it's Monsieur d'Erlen *they* want. But they'll certainly take Monsieur Thierry too, if they find him."

"Ferrand!" said Claudine, feeling quite sick.

"The one who swore to send Monsieur d'Erlen to the guillotine!" gasped out Seraphine.

"Oh, no!" cried Laurent, horrified.

"Rémy," said Claudine, pulling herself together, "drink some wine while I run and get my thick cloak. We can get there in a few minutes."

As she hurried up the next flight of stairs she heard someone behind her and found it was Seraphine.

"Of course I'm coming too!" she said breathlessly, and together they rushed to scramble into their outdoor clothes.

Claudine put on her big hooded cloak over the top of her pelisse, not merely for warmth but to hide herself in. She put on the thickest shoes and seized warm gloves.

When they went down again they found Laurent button-
ing on his greatcoat, determined to accompany them.

As they went out into the street it was beginning to get
dark. It was very cold, for there was a strong wind blowing,
but it was not actually raining or snowing – it had done one or
the other most days lately.

"Where is Monsieur de Trévires?" Rémy asked, as they
went, heads down against the wind, across the main street
outside the Judge's house.

"At the Republican headquarters," said Claudine.

They reached Frau Müller's house within ten minutes and
it was she who opened the door, startled to see such a party of
people outside. But she recognised Claudine and let them in.

"You've heard about your uncle then, mademoiselle?" she
said. "I didn't think there would have been time. Did Monsieur Gabry call, on his way to fetch the doctor?"

"What? My uncle?" said Claudine. "Is he worse?"

"Oh, my dear little lady, he's had another of those dreadful
attacks, bringing up blood . . . he's very weak."

"My cousin Thierry – where is he?" Claudine asked.

"He's with your poor uncle," said Frau Müller. "Monsieur Gabry went for the doctor – I thought it was him come
back, when you knocked."

Claudine saw Willibrord coming up the back stairs.

"Oh Willibrord, the French have found out you're here,"
she said. "Captain Ferrand from Luxembourg – we must get
Monsieur de Ravanger away."

The narrow passage was full of anxious people. Willibrord,
in great alarm, looked into the sick room and then let her in.

Xavier de Lamerle, pale and exhausted, was lying on the
bed, but his eyes were open. Thierry, who had been wiping
his face with a cloth, turned around. He was in his shirt
sleeves.

"Thierry," Claudine said, putting her hand on his arm, "I
am so sorry about my dear uncle, but you must leave this
house at once."

"I can't possibly leave him at this moment," said Thierry.

Willibrord began to urge him and the next moment Rémy
had made his way into the room and was pouring out his
story. Thierry kept saying, "Yes. Yes, I see." But he stayed
close by the bed.

Xavier had understood what was going on. "Go, Thierry,

go," he said, feebly. "I do not think I shall last this night . . .
The French can do nothing to me now. God bless you – go."

Thierry always made up his mind quickly. Now he rolled
down his sleeves and picked up his coat from the back of a
chair.

"Yes, I see I must go," he said. "But Rémy, will you find
Monsieur de Trévires? He will see that Monsieur de Lamerle
is treated with humanity."

"Rémy is terribly tired," said Seraphine.

"I can do it," said Rémy at once. He would have done
anything for Thierry de Ravanger.

"Good lad," said Thierry, shaking his hand.

Rémy was off at once.

"Now, how are we to warn Gabry?" Thierry said. "Willi,
where's Norbert?"

"Here, monsieur," said Norbert, who had come down
from the attics with Lisel, to see what all the noise was about.

"Norbert, will you and Josy scout round and try to catch
Monsieur Gabry on his way back?" said Thierry. "Lisel, my
dear, quickly pack your things, We must all be off and out of
Trier as soon as we can. We will take the path along the
heights, follow the Moselle to the Rhine. We had once
thought of a boat but there's no time to arrange that. Norbert!"

Norbert turned back; he had been already on his way.

"Tell Gabry not to come back here but to meet us on the
way. Let us make a rendezvous beyond Riol – at that place
where you can see down to the river – before the ferry at
Mehring. He knows. We'll wait there till we're all met.
Willibrord and I will bring Lisel and as much stuff as we can
carry. We'll have to travel light anyway, walking."

"Yes, monsieur."

Norbert asked pardon as he went, squeezed past everyone
in the passage, kissed Lisel as she came, crying, after him,
and vanished into the oncoming night. But Josy, Willibrord's son, could not be found.

"He's probably in the tavern across the road," said Willibrord. "He's been earning a bit, washing up there."

"We'll pick him up," said Thierry. "Go and pack, Willi –
the fewest possible things." He turned back to the bed and
knelt down beside it. "My dearest uncle, give me your bles-
sing," he said, bending his head down.

Very weakly the sick priest raised his hand, making a feeble sign of the cross with it, and then laying it on his nephew's head. The whispered Latin words were almost inaudible.

Thierry got up, bent forward and kissed his uncle's forehead with affection and then turned to go.

Mathilde had appeared in the doorway and she came in now and said, "I will sit with Monsieur de Lamerle."

Everyone else went out of the room and the girls and Laurent were taken by Frau Müller into the front parlour. Thierry hurried upstairs to put on his boots and coat.

No time had been wasted, they had all been as quick as they could in carrying out Thierry's directions, and yet just as he came back into the parlour there was a crashing on the door and shouts of, "Open in the name of the Republic!"

Willibrord appeared with a pack on his back and an old tricorne hat on his head. "Seigneur, out at the back," he said. *"Vite, Vite!"*

Thierry glanced at Claudine who said quickly, "We're all right, because of Papa. Go on, Thierry, go – goodbye."

As he went into the passage they heard Frau Müller open a window upstairs. "What do you want, you Frenchmen?" she demanded. "I'm a respectable widow, I am, can't let soldiers into my house after dark."

"You come down and open up, or it will be the worse for you," shouted a loud harsh voice.

"It's Ferrand," Claudine whispered. "Ferrand himself."

"Whether you know it or not, dame, you are harbouring traitors!" Ferrand called up. "We've got your place surrounded so open up, if you don't want your door broken in."

Frau Müller slammed down the window and came slowly, muttering in German, down the stairs. As she passed the parlour, she said, "Can't keep them out any longer, I'm afraid."

Rifle butts were already crashing on the door when she unbolted it. In a few moments Gaston Ferrand, in uniform, and his soldiers crowded inside the house.

"Search it – top to bottom," he ordered, and walked into the parlour.

He recognised Claudine and her sister at once.

"Mademoiselle de Trévires! Is your father here? Surely not, in a house that harbours rebels and traitors!"

"No, he is not here," said Claudine. "Frau Müller is not a rebel. I am staying with my aunt, not far away."

She tried to sound merely surprised, not frightened, but her knees were shaking.

Seraphine said, "Who are you looking for, Captain Ferrand? Surely you are outside your department here?"

"Yes, and had to waste precious time getting permission to carry out this raid," said Ferrand. "We are after that cursed aristocrat, known as Le Cicatrisé, who gave us the slip after we caught him at your school a couple of months ago or more. Have you seen him?"

"Is he in Trèves, then?" said Seraphine innocently. She was much better at it, Claudine thought, than herself.

But they were interrupted by shouts at the back of the house and presently some of the soldiers came into the passage dragging with them Thierry and Willibrord, who had evidently been caught before they had got through the alley behind the house. They had made a struggle for it; both were dishevelled and panting and Thierry was covered in mud.

But Gaston Ferrand, peering at him, said at once, "I've seen you before. I have it! The music master at Villerange."

"Quite right. Citoyen Capitaine," said Thierry, breathless but polite. "I am Henri Théry, and I don't know why your men should arrest me. I have my papers." He tried to put his hand in his pocket, but the men were holding his arms by the elbows.

"I don't want your papers," Ferrand said. "Whatever your name may be, it was you who made my men half drunk that night at Villerange – so that Desroux was killed and we lost Le Cicatrisé. Where is he?"

"Why should you think I know?" countered Thierry.

Gaston Ferrand gave a snort of impatience. "Well, we shall soon have him, if he is here."

Soldiers were stamping up and down the flights of stairs, crashing into all the rooms with fixed bayonets or drawn cutlasses. Claudine heard Paulette shrieking and saw Mathilde come out of the back room and run upstairs, calling out, "Paulette! It's all right. Maman is coming!"

It was a narrow but tall house and it took some time for the soldiers to go all over it. Presently Lisel was brought in, still carrying her bundle, looking scared but not mishandled. The little parlour was now crammed with people and there were soldiers on guard in the passage as well as in the street outside.

At last the sergeant came back to report.

"Le Cicatrisé is not here, *mon capitaine*."

Gaston Ferrand swore. "And what have you found – besides the women?"

"There have been several men in the house," said the man. "Beds, clothes, all there. They must have had warning."

"Clothes?" said Ferrand. "See if there's anything he could have worn – he's taller than most."

The sergeant saluted and went to the door. Then he turned back.

"And there's a dead man in the back room," he said.

"Dead!" gasped Seraphine. "He's ill, not dead."

"It's our uncle, Captain Ferrand," said Claudine. "May we go to him?"

Ferrand allowed it and Claudine went along the passage, Seraphine and Laurent following her.

It was true. Their uncle was dead. He was lying on his back on the bed with a wooden crucifix clasped in his hands. His eyes were closed and the mould of his thin pale face was set in an expression of tranquillity.

Claudine gazed at him as he lay there, one candle in its earthenware stick standing by the bed. It seemed strange that he had died alone, so quietly, while no one noticed, no one was there. He had escaped the prison of the world altogether.

"May he rest in peace," whispered Claudine, tears in her eyes. "And I am sure he does."

They all made the sign of the cross before they turned to leave the room and saw the revolutionary soldiers in the passage watching them.

Xavier de Lamerle had escaped the net of pursuit, like the psalmist's bird escaping the net of the fowler, but Thierry was caught in it.

CHAPTER
SEVENTEEN

As they went back down the dark little passage to the parlour they could hear Gaston Ferrand's harsh voice once more raised in threatening demands.

"Where is that damned rebel?"

"I don't know where he is," they heard Thierry reply.

"You know something," retorted Ferrand. "When was he last here? Has he had warning? Come on, now, out with it."

"Why should you think Frau Müller's lodgers know all about each other?" said Thierry.

"Don't try to put me off!" shouted Ferrand, losing his temper. "My men have found clothes of his upstairs. You were attempting flight. Does that rebel know we are after him?"

"I don't know," said Thierry.

Although this was a true answer, it enraged Ferrand, who struck him across the face. It was a gesture of impatience rather than of calculated brutality, but Seraphine gave a shriek.

"Oh! You brute, to hit a man who can't hit back!" she cried, pushing past Claudine into the room. "Captain Ferrand, I would not have thought it of you!"

Ferrand looked taken aback. "Citoyenne, this fellow has provoked me beyond endurance with his evasions," he said. "How can he deny that he knows something of Le Cicatrisé when we have found clothes that could only be his, here in this house?"

He waved his hand at the table and it gave Claudine a curious feeling to see thrown over it the suit Gabry had worn at the ball; the waistcoat, of embroidered silk, she remembered in particular.

"What, you think a rebel on the run would dress up like that?" said Seraphine scornfully. "How very unlikely! He's not the only tall man in Trier, I suppose."

"Citoyenne, as it happens, he was recognised at a ball,"

said Gaston Ferrand, restraining his temper with difficulty. "Will you kindly allow me to conduct this enquiry without interruption?"

Claudine saw Thierry smile at the discomfiture his little cousin was causing the revolutionary captain; she hoped this would not annoy him still more. But his attention was diverted by his lieutenant, a very young man, but with a sharp intelligent face, who had listened to the recent exchange in silence.

"*Mon capitaine*," he said now, "may I suggest that if Le Cicatrisé were to return he would take warning at the sight of our men? Everyone in this street knows we are here, though the people are prudently keeping indoors. If we were to march off and keep out of sight, we might get him to walk into this house as into a trap. After all, if this man is his friend, he may return to look for him."

Ferrand saw the sense of this proposal; by immediately organising the details, he made it his own. No one was to leave the lodging house, which would still be under guard, but the soldiers in the street would leave, with the two officers. Ferrand was to return by the back way, while the lieutenant posted his men inside houses at each end of the street.

"And this fellow had better be tied to his chair," ordered Ferrand, indicating Thierry. "We don't want any tricks."

Claudine anxiously watched while the soldiers pulled Thierry's arms over the back of the chair and tied them there. They had first taken off his greatcoat, for fear he would manage to wriggle out of it and his bonds as well.

"Citoyennes, please sit down," said Captain Ferrand. "No harm shall come to you, I assure you."

He went out into the street and they could hear a tremendous noise being made of the departure, to give the impression that the raid was over.

Presently Frau Müller came in with some coffee on a tray. "Come, young ladies, you need something hot," she said, and then exclaimed at the sight of Thierry roped to his chair. "Good God in heaven! What next? What have they done that for, monsieur? Dear me, it must be very uncomfortable. And how are you going to drink your coffee?"

Thierry smiled. "Perhaps Claudine will give it to me?"

Claudine jumped up and went over to him at once. As she

held the cup to his lips she whispered, "What can we do?"

"He must have had warning," Thierry replied softly in the Luxembourg dialect. "He would have been back with the doctor long since."

"What's that you're saying?" the sergeant demanded suspiciously. "No whispering. What's that jargon he's talking?"

"Luxembourgers' talk – no one can follow it but themselves," said one of the French soldiers.

Claudine was drinking her own coffee when Captain Ferrand returned, coming in from the back of the house. He took out his watch. "It's not late," he observed. "We must hope this fellow has not gone out for a night on the tiles."

He sat down and sent for a cup of Frau Müller's coffee.

It was very strange, all sitting round in the small stuffy parlour, with armed soldiers at the doors, waiting for Gabry.

Claudine had been reassured by Thierry's conviction that Gabry must have been warned all right; in fact, she was now more worried about Thierry himself. If they took him back to Luxembourg, when Gabry failed to turn up, they might discover that he was a *ci-devant* aristocrat and landowner, and then he would not stand much chance with the representatives of the People. They might even send him to the guillotine instead of Gabry, though the effect would not be the same, since he was not known in the same way as "Le Cicatrisé", hero of the peasant patriots.

Willibrord and Lisel had been taken into the kitchen to ease the congestion in the parlour. There was little talking there; Ferrand drummed on the table with his fingers, impatient for a dénouement which, as the time went on, the others expected less and less. Claudine began to wonder if Rémy had found her father and what he was doing. She half expected it to be Monsieur de Trévires who walked in from the street.

Laurent began to yawn. It was from the combination of tension and boredom, for it was not late, as Ferrand had remarked, though the tavern opposite was open, and they could hear the customers singing catches and banging their tankards on the tables. The songs were in German.

"And they're drinking Viez, I expect," said Laurent. "They seem to prefer it to wine in Trier, even Moselle wine."

"What's Viez?" said Seraphine.

"A sort of cider, made with apples," said Thierry. "Popu-

lar here for a long time, perhaps since the days of the Gallic
tribes."

Silence fell again, broken only by Ferrand's drumming.

Suddenly they heard shouts of laughter across the road,
and then somebody singing, loudly and drunkenly, the
refrain of a ballad, but not in German – in the Luxembourger
dialect.

Claudine sat as still as if she had been paralysed, for it was
like Gabry's voice. No, surely, it could not be. If he had been
sent to fetch a doctor for Thierry's dying uncle, he would
hardly have gone to drink in a tavern instead.

But in a few moments they heard staggering steps and a
muffled thump on the street door, as if the singer had landed
against it, and Gabry's voice, unmistakably his, though thic-
kened with drink, shouted, "Oh – Frau – Hanna! Good Frau
– Hanna! Let me – in!"

He rattled the latch.

Gaston Ferrand rose quietly to his feet. "I think that's our
man," he said. "And he sounds as if he's made our task easy
for us, the sot!"

"Oh! Come on!" roared Gabry, hitting the door with his
fist. "Open up – dear old – Frau!"

Ferrand made a signal to the soldiers in the passage to open
the door. As one of them did so Thierry shouted, "Look out,
Gabry! The French are here!"

The sergeant clapped his hand over Thierry's mouth,
muffling the last words, but Gabry could hardly have failed
to hear. He must have been fuddled indeed, for when the
door was flung back he was still standing on the step and the
light from the parlour streamed out and fell full on his face,
showing up the jagged red scar on his cheek that made him all
too easy to recognise.

He was certainly looking dishevelled, as if he had already
had the night out that Ferrand had scornfully conjectured.
His black hair was in a tangle and he had his coat loosely
round his shoulders, as if he had not been able to get his arms
into the sleeves on leaving his carousal in the tavern opposite.

It was only a moment that he stood there, but quite long
enough to be seen, and for him to see the tricolour cockades.

"Oh! The Sons of Liberty!" he shouted mockingly and
turned and ran down the street to the left.

His coat fell off and dark as the night was, he was plainly

visible, in his white shirt and light buff breeches, the back of his waistcoat hardly darker.

The soldiers gave chase and Ferrand, out on the step in a moment, fired his pistol.

"A miss!" cried Gabry, throwing up his arm, and he laughed.

He was running along the middle of the street but veering a bit from side to side.

Claudine had run to the door and was staring out, Seraphine beside her. "What is he doing?" she muttered, bewildered.

They heard Thierry's voice in the room behind them, speaking in dialect. "I'm afraid he's done that to draw them off from here," he said. "Laurent, have you a pocket knife, or can you undo these cords?"

There were no soldiers left in the room. Ferrand had walked a few paces down the street.

"Does Gabry know there are soldiers at the end of the road?" Thierry wondered as he struggled, with Laurent's aid, to free his arms.

It was soon only too clear that he did not. The lieutenant's party came tumbling out from their hiding place at the sound of the pistol shot and spread out, barring the way.

Gabry instantly doubled back, so quickly that he took his pursuers by surprise and dodged between them, running fast along the side of the street opposite the lodging house.

Claudine was suddenly reminded of his flight in the house at Villerange. He was going to be caught again between the two parties of the enemy. And indeed he had scarcely got past the tavern when the French soldiers emerged at the other end of the street, where the lamp on the main road showed up their arms and tricolour badges.

Ferrand was standing, watching. "Ha! We've got you this time!" he shouted triumphantly. "Assassin!"

Claudine was shaking. In imagination she already saw Gabry trapped between the advancing soldiers, captured.

But he cried, "Oh! You've got to work harder than that for my blood, Citoyen Guillotine!"

And he ran through the open door of the tavern.

Ferrand swore. But he was quick to order the oncoming soldiers to surround the inn; some of them ran through the stableyard to get to the back, and Claudine, her heart thump-

ing, feared that Gabry could hardly have got through the
building more quickly than they had got round to the back of
it.

Suddenly she heard a Luxembourger voice behind her.
"Shut the door, mademoiselle. Shut him out, that blood-
thirsty captain."

It was Norbert Wagener.

She was too surprised to obey; he shut the door himself and
bolted it.

"Norbert! What's up?" Thierry demanded.

He had got free of his bonds and was standing up, rubbing
his elbows.

"Monsieur Thierry, it's his plan," said Norbert. "He
knew they would go after him, if they once saw him. You are
to come with us, Josy and me, at once. We meet at that place
beyond Riol. If he gets away from them."

His voice was heavy with gloom. "We didn't know they
had ambushes out," he said. "We've been in the tavern all
this time. Monsieur Gabry met that young fellow, Monsieur
de Trévires' secretary, and he warned him."

"Rémy did? Good!" said Thierry. "But Norbert, we can't
just run away and leave Gabry in this fix."

"No, but we must get out of this house," said Norbert.

"How can we do that?" Laurent asked. He had been
listening anxiously. "What about the guards downstairs and
out at the back? How did you get in?"

"Through the cellars, and that's how we'll get out," said
Norbert. "The soldiers in the back alley won't know anything about it. As for the two downstairs, Josy and I have
locked them in the broom cupboard, tied up with Frau
Müller's washing line."

"Oh, wonderful!" cried Laurent, grinning.

"We can't go over to the tavern, now that it's full of
Frenchmen," said Norbert. "We'll go to the house next
door. It's another lodging house and Frau Müller has already
gone to warn them. She says they'll help."

"But I don't understand about the cellars," said Thierry.

"They go right under the road, Seigneur," said Norbert.
"Luckily that cleverboots, Captain Ferrand, doesn't know it
either. Of course there are doors, but the tavern people let us
through and Frau Müller has the key to the one between her
and her neighbour."

Thierry had already put on his greatcoat. Now he turned to kiss Seraphine and Claudine goodbye, with another kiss and a pat on the shoulder for Laurent.

"Be sure we won't desert Gabry," he said, "but we can do more once we're free."

Norbert put his hand in his pocket. "Mademoiselle," he said shyly to Claudine, "he sent this to you."

He held out to her Gabriel's ring.

As she took it she remembered so vividly the time she had kept it before and how she had given it back, that intense feeling made it difficult to thank Norbert. But she managed to say, "If you see him, tell him how happy I am to keep it for him."

Norbert looked sadly at her with his large brown eyes and she knew that he had small hope of seeing his master again. But he said nothing.

When he and Thierry had gone down the cellar stairs the three young cousins looked at each other.

"They've probably caught him by now," Seraphine said despondently.

"Let's go upstairs," said Laurent. "Then we can look out of the window."

He led the way, the girls following. They ran up the first flight and into the room which had been shared by Thierry and Gabry. The soldiers had pulled the beds apart, flung open cupboards and drawers, and tossed everything about.

Seraphine had brought up a lighted candle from the parlour and this gave a flickering illumination. She put it down on a chest as Laurent opened the shutters and then the windows, which also opened inwards. Cold air rushed in, the girls shivered and the candle-flame bent smoking away from the blast. Laurent hastily pushed the casements together again.

Standing crowded in the window embrasure, they peered down the narrow street. Most of the light outside came from the tavern, which as well as the lamp over the door had another at the stable arch. Its doors too were wide open and many of the windows were lighted. There was a lot of shouting and banging of doors and feet over there; it was an even noisier search than the one in the lodging house had been.

"Oh, how can we escape them?" Claudine whispered, clutching Gabry's ring in her hand, close against her breast.

Suddenly Seraphine said, "There's Rémy down there – coming out of the yard." She opened the window again and called out, "Rémy! Up here, look!"

He looked round and about and then caught sight of her waving hand and came quickly across the street. He stood under the window looking up and said in the Luxembourg dialect, "Thank God you are safe, at any rate. Has – your cousin got away?"

"From here, yes," said Seraphine. "Norbert told us that you warned Gabry."

"I felt he – Monsieur Thierry – would wish it," said Rémy, making it clear that his hostility to Gabry himself was unchanged.

"Have you seen our father?" Claudine asked.

Rémy shook his head. "He had left by the time I had arrived at the headquarters," he said. "I heard about this raid there and came back to see if I could help Monsieur Thierry. I thought he must be over there in the tavern, but it's only the other one." His eyes were on Claudine. "He can't get away this time, mademoiselle – the place is surrounded."

"I must shut the window," said Laurent. "It's too cold for my cousins." ·

Rémy nodded. He turned round, looking towards the inn, but stayed there below.

"Look! Look!" cried Laurent suddenly. "Isn't that Gabry? Up there? At the dormer window?"

When she looked across, Claudine knew instantly that it was. Gabry had opened the window and was climbing up on to the sill. He stood up on it and then, holding on to the wooden weatherboard of the eaves, edged himself round the corner so that he was standing on the steep slope of the tiled roof. Then he shifted his handgrip from the eaves to the coping, so that he was leaning against the side of the dormer.

"He can't be seen there from inside," said Laurent, excitedly.

"But the windows aren't properly closed," said Seraphine.

Gabry had pulled them shut after him, as well as he could, but as the catch was inside, the gusty wind had blown them open again.

"Oh, there's someone in the room!" Claudine said, in an anguish of anxiety.

A soldier came up to the window. He had a musket with a fixed bayonet in his hand. He shouted to someone behind him and then leant out of the dormer, and saw Gabry's foot. He let out a triumphant cry and stabbed at the fugitive's leg with his bayonet but it was an awkward angle; he missed, and nearly fell head-first.

Gabry, realising that he was discovered, hauled himself up till he could sit on the eave of the dormer.

The soldiers inside were shouting and gesticulating to each other. It was plain that they wanted to catch their man, they too must climb out on the roof and after a few minutes one of them began to do so. Gabry leant over and hit his clinging hand hard with his fist.

The man yelled, wavered, and managed to drop back inside the window.

Laurent gave a sort of cheer, Rémy turned round.

"What is he doing?" he asked in the dialect. "The French say he came back drunk."

"Of course he isn't drunk," said Laurent indignantly. "He came back to lure them away, so that Thierry could escape – that's what Norbert told us."

Rémy said nothing but stood staring up at the distant figure astride the dormer roof.

Gabry was obviously waiting for the next attempt to get out from the window below him. Instead, another window was opened, further along.

"*Look out!*" yelled Laurent, at the top of his voice.

He had seen the barrel of the gun there, just before the man behind it fired.

His cry was hardly in time to warn Gabry, yet he moved at the sound of it and the bullet hit the roof, for a bit of tile jumped off.

Realising that he made a target from the other window, Gabry got himself off the dormer eave, spreadeagled on the steep slope above it and clawed his way up towards the main coping of the high gabled roof.

Claudine was so terrified that she felt as if her heart refused to beat. Surely he could not get up there! Surely he would be shot before he did.

But the man at the other window had to change places with a comrade whose musket was loaded, and before this second man could take aim, Gabry had succeeded in scrambling up to the top of the roof, where they could see him looking over the other side. Up there, the man with the musket could not get within aim of him unless he himself climbed out of the window and this he proceeded to do – but he handed back his gun first and it was some minutes before he could take it again and aim over the top of the dormer.

In those few minutes Gabry had drawn himself into a crouching position on top of the main coping of thick rounded tiles. Moving carefully he stood up, balancing himself with his arms, and then suddenly walked quickly along the perilous ridge towards the chimney stack. The musketeer fired but his ball went over the roof behind Gabry.

Then he reached the chimney-stack and swung himself round behind it. Now no marksman could get him unless he too was prepared to go roof-climbing.

Claudine found that she had been holding her breath. She let it out in a sigh that was almost a sob.

"I say, how cool!" Laurent cried, in admiration. "It's like his fencing – such balance and control."

Then they heard Ferrand's harsh voice. He had come out of the tavern into the street and was shouting up to the men in the attics, ordering them to get out on the roof.

"He's not armed – take pistols but take him alive if you can, he can't get away. The place is surrounded."

Claudine felt it was unbearable. Whatever Gabry did, he must be caught in the end and now there was more agonising suspense to be endured, in the fear that he would be shot dead or wounded and perhaps fall to his death in his efforts to escape the men closing in round him.

"It's not fair," she heard Seraphine muttering, shivering beside her in the cold air which blew in from the open window.

But when Laurent offered to shut it both of them demurred.

The roofs of the inn were on different levels, for it had been built on to at various times. When he had walked along the coping, Gabry had been on the highest ridge, but from where they were they could presently see him climbing on to a slightly lower roof, though he was still invisible to the men who had got out of the second dormer window and, not daring his catlike feats, were creeping round the parapet which carried the gutters.

"When they get round the corner, they'll see him," Seraphine said.

"But they won't be able to get down to the next roof from there," said Laurent. "Unless they jump, and they don't look any too happy roof-climbing, to me."

"But if he goes much nearer to the edge of that second roof, the men in the road will see him and fire at him from there," said Seraphine.

Ferrand had posted men below with muskets ready, in case the rebel presented a target.

"It's quite a long shot and an awkward one," said Laurent. "He's high up and it's round the corner, above the alley."

A narrow alley ran between the inn and the next group of buildings, a great block of town houses some of which fronted the main road which ran past at the end of the side street. Roofs tilted there like tents; there were gable ends patterned with beams; woodwork, guttering, weathervanes, stuck up in a man-made forest.

Intent on getting down the steep slope of tiles safely, Gabry did not see the men coming along the parapet above and behind him, on the higher level, till the leader, excited at spotting his quarry, fired off his pistol.

It was too far for accurate aiming and the bullet fell short, but now the soldiers in the street began firing too.

"Oh, if only he had on darker clothes!" Seraphine said. Gabry's light breeches and white shirt made him an easy target.

Laurent said, "I expect he took off his coat so that they could see him, as he meant to draw them off from here. But of course he only meant to lead them a run through the town. He didn't know he was going to be cornered like this."

Gabriel had reached the edge of the second roof, which flattened out a little towards its gutter and here once more he stood up, carefully balancing, apparently ignoring both the musketry and the pistol shots.

Claudine had not said a word; she could not. Not only were her eyes fixed on Gabry; she felt identified with his every movement. She had guessed what he was going to do before Laurent said it.

"My God! He's going to jump across!"

The narrow alley presented a gap of only a few feet but it was a yawning chasm and the roofs each side were old and uneven and steep. Moreover if he leaped it, Gabry would have to take off from a standing position. He could not make a run at it.

"Oh no, don't!" whispered Seraphine, clasping her hands together. "Don't risk it, Gabry! He'll fall down and be killed."

But the next moment they saw him bend his knees and then he had made the spring, out over the black blank, and landed, slipping, on the roof the other side, catching at the weather-boarding of a gable.

It looked as if he were going to slide off, but the board held, and his grip held till he had found firm footing, and then, almost before the watchers realised that he had safely done it, he was scrambling up between the gables, he was swinging round another chimney-stack, and vanished into the dark jumble of roof tops.

"He's done it!" cried Laurent triumphantly.

In the street they could hear Ferrand, furious and suddenly afraid of losing his prey yet once more, yelling orders to his men.

Rémy looked up and called, "Will you let me in?"

Seraphine ran down to open the door. Claudine leant against the wall, feeling dizzy and faint. Her hand was hurting. Opening it, she saw Gabriel's ring. She had unconsciously gripped it so hard it had made a red mark on her palm. She stared at her own hand, hardly aware of it.

Gabriel had a chance, just a chance, of escaping after all.

CHAPTER
EIGHTEEN

WHEN Claudine went down the stairs she heard Rémy saying, "I think I had better escort you back to the Judge's house."

She knew then, quite suddenly, what she was going to do.

"Rémy, I am not coming," she said. "I am going after Cousin Thierry – just in case Gabry gets away."

She saw him look up, puzzled and frowning. "Mademoiselle Claudine, how can you do that?"

"She is going to marry Monsieur d'Erlen," said Seraphine. "That is, if he is not captured."

"Marry him?" said Rémy slowly. "Is it as settled as that?"

"Yes," said Claudine and she held out her hand, showing him Gabry's signet ring. "He sent me this by Norbert as – as a sign between us, or a farewell token, for he must have known how dangerous his plan was."

She was uncertain of Rémy's reaction, knowing the romantic admiration he had cherished for herself and his old hatred of Gabriel d'Erlen.

But now he said, "Do you mean he knew you would marry him if he were free, and yet risked capture to save Monsieur Thierry?" And when she assented he remarked, "Well then, I do not think he is so undeserving of you as he seemed to be."

Claudine smiled. "I am glad, if you don't hate him any longer, Rémy," she said.

"But you can't go after Monsieur Thierry alone," said Rémy. "I will escort you."

Claudine was relieved at this offer, though she had been ready to risk going alone.

But now Seraphine suddenly realised what her decision would mean. "Claudine! Are you really going away – right away, over the Rhine?"

"If Gabry goes," said Claudine.

"But if – supposing he is caught?" Seraphine said.

"Then I shall come back," said Claudine. "But now I must hurry, or I'll not catch up Thierry, and I don't know the way to Riol." She came down the rest of the stairs and hugged her sister. "Darling Seraphine, if I don't come back soon you will know he is safe and that I am happy. And of course we will meet again – when Luxembourg is free."

"Let me come too," Seraphine begged. "I'd like to be an *émigrée*."

"What, and leave our parents with no children? Oh no, Seraphine, you can't do that! Besides, I rely on you to explain my flight to maman . . . that is, if Gabry escapes."

So it was settled, for there was no time to lose, and Rémy and Claudine hurried down the lower stairs. Frau Müller was just coming up from the cellars.

"They've already started," she told them, when Claudine hastily explained her purpose. "Here, take the lantern and the key – leave the key in the door, and I'll come back and lock it."

"Which way have they gone?" Rémy asked.

"Across to the tavern cellars," Frau Müller said. "The French have all left that place now. Next thing is, someone will be sent back for that Henri Théry, or whatever his name is. Oh! that's them! No, it isn't! It's the pair those two Luxembourgers shut in my broom cupboard!"

Thumping and muffled shouts were sounding from the back of the house.

Frau Müller burst out laughing. "Oh, what an evening! Did you see that Monsieur Gabry climbing about on the roofs like a mountain goat? We watched from my neighbour's windows."

She was still talking as they went down the cellar stairs into mustiness and darkness.

Claudine was glad indeed to have Rémy's company. They turned left, found the door to the neighbouring cellar, and unlocked it, leaving the key in. But after stumbling about over heaps of fuel, when they found the door under the road it was locked, and did not yield when Rémy kicked it.

However, he was not to be beaten so easily, and looked about till he found a chopper, and used it to prise open the door, while Claudine, shivering the cold and excitement, held the lantern.

The tavern cellars were very extensive and confusing and

Claudine was greatly relieved when she heard out of the darkness, Lisel's voice raised in a penetrating whisper: "It's the French!" she was saying in alarm. "They're after us, Norbert!"

"Lisel! It's me, Claudine!"

A few minutes later they met round a corner. Thierry, with old Willibrord and his son Josy, were a little further ahead, but came back when they saw who had come. Claudine once more explained her intentions and Thierry agreed that Gabry now had some chance of escaping. "Though, heaven knows, he has enough men chasing him," he said soberly.

"Did you see him on the roof?" Rémy asked.

Thierry smiled. "Yes – and I couldn't help remembering how he climbed one of the churches in Luxembourg for a bet, when he was a wild youngster, about your age, Rémy, I dare say. He put his hat on one of the pinnacles to prove he had got there."

Then he told Rémy he must return to the lodging-house and take Seraphine and Laurent home. "You had better go up into the tavern and cross the road overground – Josy will show you the way. You'll be able to catch us up, Josy. We will look after Claudine now. You have done very well, Rémy. I thank you for warning Gabry, for Norbert tells me it saved him from running straight into Ferrand's company – Norbert himself was too late. He had to sneak into the tavern and found Gabry already there. It was especially good of you, because we all know Monsieur d'Erlen is no favourite of yours."

"I think better of him, after tonight," said Rémy. "And I hope he will get safe away."

He said goodbye, holding Claudine's hand for a moment, with a wistful look. "I must wish, for your sake, that I don't see you again too soon," he said. "May all go well for you, Mademoiselle Claudine."

She thanked him, and he went off with Josy, through the dim cobwebbed tunnels.

"Come on, Seigneur, come on," said Willibrord impatiently. "Josy can follow – he knows the way."

And so they started off once more, going through cellars and passages under the road, coming up at last in a yard, from which they were able to slip into an alley, as narrow as that which Gabry had jumped.

Glancing up at the slice of night sky far above, Claudine shuddered, thinking of that frightening leap. In the distance she could hear a dog barking, but no shots. Was he safe?

They got out of the city without difficulty and began the long walk. It was seven or eight miles to Riol and there Thierry decided it was safe to put up for the night. The people of the Moselle country were all friendly; to them the revolutionary French were the enemy, who had taken their barges to make pontoon bridges, or cut them up for firewood, seized the barge horses to cart army drays or to provide horse meat, reduced the busy traffic of the river to mere fishing boats and ferries and perhaps worst of all, sacked the monasteries and insulted the shrines of St. Nicholas on their way through to the Rhine.

Riol itself was in the orchard country, a Viez centre. Ancient country, land of her distant ancestors, and Thierry's – and Gabry's, in all probability.

She shared a room and a bed with Lisel. "Oh mademoiselle," said Lisel, stroking her hair affectionately, "pray God Monsieur le Comte has escaped his enemies! I am glad he knows you love him. Norbert has told me how much he has been thinking of you, ever since he first saw you, at Villerange. He told me then, Norbert says: 'That is the girl for me – but she won't have me.' That's how it seemed to him, then."

Claudine was comforted by Lisel's simple sentiments. And she was so tired that in spite of her anxiety, she slept the rest of the night.

The next morning they were worried because Josy had not yet caught up with them, but Willibrord insisted on going on.

"Josy knows his way," he said. "He's not daring, that boy. He's probably stopped the night somewhere behind us."

He proved to be right, for later that day when they were walking high above the Moselle among firs and pines, Willibrord saw his son toiling up the path behind them. So they sat down in a clearing to wait for him.

From here they could see right down to the river and in the distance the village of Meyring on the opposite bank, where the ferry carried travellers across the Moselle and the path continued on the other side. They were almost, Thierry said, at the place where they had arranged to wait for each other, and where he was now hoping that Gabry would join them.

It was cold here on the north-faced slopes and the ground was covered in snow. The strong wind had dropped but the airs sighed through the bluish needles of the pines, far above their heads. The sun shone, a pale wintry gleam, on the far side of the river, but here they were in shadow.

They sat on some sawn tree-trunks, huddled in their coats, and Claudine was glad she had her thick hooded cloak as well.

As Josy came towards them they saw an expression of sadness on his fresh rosy face; he was only twenty, small and sturdy and squareheaded like his father, with brown hair growing thick and short.

"What is the matter, my son?" said Willibrord, standing up.

"Oh, father, they've got him," said Josy, breathless, speaking in the Luxembourg dialect. He looked at Thierry. "Seigneur, our Monsieur Gabry is taken by the French."

They all stared at him. Somehow they had been confident that Gabry had got away.

"They managed to shoot him down?" said Thierry at last. "He's wounded?"

"I don't think so, Seigneur," said Josy.

"Sit down and tell us what you know," said Thierry,

Josy sat down. His eyebrows were crinkled into a frown of distress. "When I took that Rémy Lefèvre up to the tavern, Seigneur," he began, "we heard a dog barking like a mad thing and the potboy came running in saying he was dead, Monsieur Gabry was dead – they all knew him by name. He'd fallen and was killed."

Thierry quickly took Claudine's hand in his.

"Mademoiselle, he isn't, of course," said Josy. "But that's what this boy said, and we ran out with him, both of us, and more of the inn people. We ran up the alley to the other end of that block of buildings he jumped on to from the roof, where there's a little cobbled place, you may remember, with a water trough and a fountain. There's a lamp on the corner there too, on an iron bracket. And there we saw Monsieur Gabry lying on the ground, and we too thought he was dead for a moment, but then we saw the French tying his wrists with cord, so we knew he was only unconscious. They must have heard the dog barking – it was still barking and jumping about behind a high wall, we could hear its chain rattling. It was terrible bad luck. Monsieur Gabry must have come down just where that dog was and wakened it. I don't know just what happened, but he must have fallen, getting away from it. He must have hit his head and knocked himself out, for it wasn't a great height."

"What wretched luck, when he had got away with much worse risks," said Thierry.

"Then that Ferrand appeared," said Josy. "By that time, Monsieur Gabry was coming round, but I don't think he quite knew what was happening. He is usually so quick, you know, but he didn't do anything, just let him pull him up to his feet, and then leant against the wall. One of them held a pistol against his chest and another held the end of the rope they'd tied his hands with."

"And what were you doing all this time?" Norbert demanded. "Why didn't you try to help Monsieur Gabry get away?"

Josy's red face turned redder still. "There were so many French, and all armed," he said. "Some were keeping the crowd back with bayonets – and they were only householders, come out to look, and they didn't know what was happening. I heard someone saying Monsieur Gabry was an *émigré* French aristocrat – and another that he was an Austrian spy. And when that Captain Ferrand came it did seem like that, because he was in his triumph and insulted Monsieur Gabry, calling him traitor and rebel and assassin, shouting in his face, spitting in it, one might say. He didn't take any notice. He just stared over the top of Ferrand's head."

"I know that expression of Gabry's – it's far more insulting than words," said Thierry. "It can't have made the Captain's temper any sweeter."

"What happened next?" Claudine asked, dreading to hear, yet longing to know.

"Well, Captain Ferrand sent a party to fetch you, Seigneur, whom he thought still in the lodging-house," said Josy. "There was another tavern on the corner – our nearest rival, the Boar's Head – and he went into it and called for drinks for the men who had made the capture and they all stood round waiting. They made Monsieur Gabry stand under the lamp, so as to keep watch on him. For he had got over his bump on the head and I saw him looking about – once I thought he saw me."

"And you didn't do anything!" cried Norbert in disgust.

"What could Josy have done, Norbert?" Thierry said, for the young man was looking very much ashamed. "Tell us the rest of your story, Josy. Did you wait till they actually took him away?"

Claudine guessed that Thierry was still hoping that Gabry might have given his enemies the slip, after Josy had left the scene.

"I was just wondering if I couldn't rush forward and cut him free," said Josy, "when those men, the revolutionaries, began mocking him and laughing, because of the lamp, which they called *lanterne*. It was sticking out on an iron spear, like those ones in Paris where they strung up aristocrats and royalists at the beginning of the Revolution. '*A la lanterne!*' they said, making gestures of hanging round their own throats. And then one of them threw the rope over the bar and hauled on it, so that it pulled Monsieur Gabry's arms up over his head, and they laughed at lot at that. It wasn't round his neck, of course, so he wasn't in danger of being strangled, but when they hauled on the rope till he could not keep his feet on the ground, it must have hurt. Then they'd let him down suddenly and laugh again. It was a joke to them, you see. And that Ferrand just stood in the doorway with his wine and laughed too. He didn't stop it. But then the other party came back to say you were gone, Seigneur, and that put an end to their amusement. Ferrand was annoyed, but he said, 'Well, we've got the one we want most – he's for the guillotine in Luxembourg.' And he ordered them to form up, with the prisoner in the middle and they began to march away. Of course some people followed and so did I. But Rémy Lefèvre said he was going back to take Mademoiselle Seraphine home. I think he was sorry they had caught Monsieur Gabry even though he is a Republican himself, like Monsieur de Trévires."

Norbert said restlessly, "And where have they put him?"

He was standing up, as if he was ready to walk straight back to Trier.

"I think they must have started at once for Luxembourg," said Josy. "I followed them all the way to the bridge but there was a guard set there, turning people back. So I just saw them marching off into the dark, with Monsieur Gabry in the middle of them, and one pulling him along by the rope as if he was leading a bull to market."

Nobody said anything; hope seemed eclipsed. Presently Josy added, "I came to tell you, but I couldn't get as far as Riol last night, I was so tired. I stopped at Fastrau and this morning I – I'm afraid I overslept."

Norbert made a sound expressive of disgust. "So we've wasted hours," he said. "Now, what are we going to do to rescue him, Monsieur Thierry?"

Claudine got up and walked away, stopping where she could look down to the river. She could hear discussion and argument going on behind her, for Willibrord was determined that whoever went back to Luxembourg it should not be Thierry.

"It's no good, Seigneur – they know you're what they call a traitor, even if they don't know you're the Comte d'Isenbourg. You have a duty to Madame your wife, and your little son – even to Monsieur Gabry's son, since you're almost a father to him."

Claudine heard, but she could not think about it. Her whole mind and heart were filled with the pain of knowing that Gabry was captured, that Gaston Ferrand, who had sworn to send him to the guillotine, had him in his power. She went over and over in her mind the scenes of Josy's story, feeling the agony of disappointment anew. That he should have climbed so dangerously and then fallen off a mere wall, escaped the men with guns only to fall victim to the barking of a watchdog – it was too bitter.

And although she loved Norbert for his faithful devotion, she was unable to share his hope. Was it likely that Norbert and a few loyal peasants could rescue Gabry from the fortress of Luxembourg and the hands of the French garrison? For inevitably Ferrand's party would be there before they could catch up with them. They must have had horses on the other side of the river. By now, even if they had stopped to sleep, they would be well on their way.

Claudine felt inwardly sapped of strength; she felt hollow, worn thin, dry and brittle. It was all over, this sudden love, this discovery that another person could become the centre of the world and of all her feelings and thoughts. They were going to kill Gabry and she felt her only wish was to be killed too. The wastes of life ahead without him seemed an unendurable desert.

She stood leaning against a tree staring, unseeing, down at the river. And presently her mind adverted to something her eyes had already noticed but not taken in. There was a boat down there, a small black oval sliding downstream towards Meyring, but quite close to this bank. One man was rowing and another sitting looking, and presently pointing, towards the edge. The rower began to bring the boat into the shore.

They were so far below that they were just two dark figures dwarfed by the distance. And yet somehow Claudine found herself watching with intense concentration. There was something about the way that man jumped out of the boat and pushed its nose off again, and waved to his friend.

The oarsman turned the boat upstream and began slowly rowing back the way he had come.

The other one came up from the shore, through some grassy meadowland and began to climb the hill, almost directly below the clearing.

Claudine had her hand on the tree; she almost had to hold on to it because she was trembling so violently. It looked so like . . . and yet it could not be.

Thierry came up behind her. "Claudine, we think we will go on to the hut which we originally meant for the meeting place," he began, and then broke off. His voice sounded queer as he said, "Who's that, coming up the hill?"

"He got out of a boat – there it is, going back upstream." Claudine's voice was unsteady.

The man was climbing at a steady pace through the scrubby trees in the clearing, which ran right down the side of the hill. Presently he stopped for breath and looked up. He must have seen them for he suddenly waved and called out, like a boatman: "Holla ho!" ending with a laugh.

"But it is!" cried Claudine. "It *is* Gabry!"

And she began to run straight down the hill towards him.

"Claudine!" called Thierry. "Be careful!"

He was afraid she would trip on the rough ground and fall headlong. But Claudine's feet seemed to know of themselves where to tread – and she was used to running at Hautefontaine with Seraphine.

Thierry stood by the pine tree and watched her flying

down the slope, her hood falling back and her thick golden
brown hair lifting with the speed of her going; and he
watched Gabry, climbing as fast as he could up the hill, heard
him cry, "*You* here, Claudine? It's a miracle!" and hold out
his arms to catch her as she came. And he swung her feet off
the ground.

Thierry smiled.

It was no surprise to him that Gabry had fallen in love with
Claudine, but it had surprised him that his serious, dreamy
cousin should have returned the passion so entirely. But as
they began to walk slowly up the hill again, together, with
Gabry's arm round Claudine's shoulders and hers round his
back, Thierry realised what Seraphine said men never guessed about Claudine – that she had a strong, even obstinate
character, strong with the strength of innocence and simplic-
ity. Thierry thought that Gabry would need all his nearly
twelve years of seniority to hold his own with Claudine, and
that made him smile again. In many ways his Erlen cousin,
though his own age, had always seemed younger – perhaps it
was his headlong way of living, and his ability to get himself
into trouble, always with the utmost publicity. But now,
Thierry thought, if he had the love of someone as tenacious
and honest as Claudine, his adventures might turn out more
happily.

And so he stood and waited for them and said, with a smile
as they came up, "Bless you, my children!"

"Listen to him, the old greybeard!" said Gabry, and he
clapped Thierry on the shoulder, in high spirits.

He was wearing what appeared to Claudine a curious,
almost nautical costume, which he explained had belonged to
one of the halfen, the men who had driven teams of horses
hauling barges up stream to Trier.

"It was the only suit of clothes I could borrow at Ruwer
that I could get into," he said. "The Halfen are out of work
now, poor fellows, since the French took their horses, and
the boats too. This one had taken to the hills to avoid conscription."

Gabry had on heavy nailed boots, white breeches, a blue
waistcoat and a thick jacket; a red neckerchief and a broad
felt hat completed the costume. As all the clothes were well-
worn they would not be considered strange along the length
of the Moselle.

Then Norbert and Josy came running from the clearing, amazed to see Monsieur Gabry not only free but apparently well and cheerful; Josy in particular stared at him as if he were a ghost.

Gabriel did not realise till they told him that Josy had witnessed his capture; he had not noticed him in the crowd last night.

"Well! And I was hoping to pretend I got clean away!" he said. "Instead of getting caught by the heels – literally, by that savage beast of a dog – so that I lost my footing and went over the wall head-first."

"But how did you get away from them, monsieur?" Josy said, still gaping. "I saw them march you off over Trier bridge."

"Yes, and I felt so desperate then I thought I would risk drowning rather than go on with our friend Ferrand," said Gabry. "I saw a boat coming with two men and a pile of nets on board, upstream of the bridge, and so I gave a great pull on my rope and got it away from the soldier who held it. I jumped up on to the parapet and over into the river before they knew what I was doing. I was carried under the arch, of course, just as I meant, and I managed to hang on to the stones at the side till the boat's nose came in, and then I caught hold of the gunwale – both hands tied together, but I did it. I only meant to hide alongside, but those good fellows pulled me in at once and threw the nets over me, and when we came out the other side they gesticulated back towards the bridge, shouting in German that there was a man under there. So off we went at a good speed, leaving old Ferrand cursing and ordering his men to get boats and search for me – or my body. It was funny; we had a good laugh, later on."

"Funny!" said Claudine, with a shiver.

Gabriel put his arm round her again. "Funny afterwards," he said, "like so many things that are frightening at the time."

"And all this was happening last night!" exclaimed Thierry. "So you stopped at Ruwer, Josy got to Fastrau, and we were at Riol. Well! What a game!"

"I went the long way round in taking the river today," said Gabry. "It makes such great loops. But to tell you the truth, I didn't feel like a long walk! I'm as stiff as if I'd ridden a race after not having been on a horse for months."

"You come and sit down, Monsieur le Comte," said Willibrord, "and have something to eat."

He had built a fire and got bread and sausage out of his knapsack, and a bottle of wine. "Moselle, not Viez," he said, scornfully.

They all sat down again on the sawn tree-trunks and Claudine felt as if it were a dream. Or was it last night's wild chase which had been the dream? It gave her a curious feeling to recall that she had heard the dog barking in the distance as they had emerged from the cellars, and had not known it was barking at Gabry, nor of what was happening to him, caught by Ferrand's men. Now here she was sitting beside him, in the woods once more, but not their own beechwoods. Suddenly she noticed that his wrists were roughly bandaged.

"Gabry, why this?" she asked, laying a finger lightly on the linen strips, under cover of a discussion among the others as to how long it would take to reach Meyring.

"Oh, that good wife of the Ruwer fisherman, she would do it," he replied. "The skin was rubbed off by the rope, that's all. It will soon mend. This keeps the dirt out."

Claudine remembered Josy's tale of the rope being hauled over the bar of the street lamp. She leant her head against his shoulder. "I know what they did to you," she whispered. "Josy told us."

"Josy had no business to tell you," said Gabry, frowning. "I suppose he is too young or too stupid to guess how a woman might feel." Then he gave a chuckle. "I bet old Ferrand wishes he *had* hanged me *à la lanterne*, now!"

Thierry heard the last remark and turned to him. "I expect the rope would have broken," he said. "For you really do have the devil's own luck, Gabry, as they say of your family."

"So long as he doesn't carry me down below before my wedding!" said Gabry. "That is, if my angel of Liberty is going to consent to a wedding. Don't you republicans go in for something quite different? I, Citoyen, take thee, Citoyenne . . . to be ever faithful to the Republic, one and indivisible."

Claudine had to laugh. "But Gabry, you know I am not as republican as that," she said. "Of course I want to be married in church."

"Of course she does," said Thierry, amused. "And I shall make sure it's done properly before I go down the Rhine on my way to England – while you, I suppose, will go the other way, to join the Archduke Charles?"

The future, even so soon ahead, still seemed unreal to Claudine. She could not believe she was not going back to Hautefontaine, could not imagine her life beyond the Rhine, married to Gabry. When they left the clearing and walked on, she moved still in a dream. Gabry had come back, almost as if from the dead. The nightmare of pursuit was over, for though they were still in the territory of the enemy, they were already far outside Ferrand's district. They were nearly free and yet when Thierry spoke of their going opposite ways, she felt that she was going into unknown country, to live among strangers.

As they went towards the ferry stage, Gabry was talking of the presents he wanted him to take to England, to his own son Ludovic and to Petronella, Thierry's wife, and their baby son.

"Though what will they care when they see you safe?" he said. "You are the only present Petronella will want."

"If that is true, it will still be you who sends it to her," said Thierry. He was walking the other side of Gabriel. "For without your quixotic action, *mon cousin*, it's likely she would never have seen me again."

"Quixotic? Fooh! You would have done the same for me, or anyone," said Gabry.

Thierry smiled, glancing down at the stout stick Willibrord had cut for him. "I could not have done the *same*," he said. "I am not such a tomcat on the rooftops as you are."

Claudine felt it unkind of him to refer to the accident which Gabriel had caused, long ago, until she realised he had done it on purpose.

"And now you can forgive yourself for that, Gabry," Thierry said quietly.

"That I never can – it is different," Gabriel said gravely, but Claudine thought his face was less strained than when the fact had been brought to his memory before. She could still recall the shadow that had come over his face when, not knowing who he was, she had spoken of the young Comte d'Erlen, who had pushed his cousin off a wall and lamed him for life. And she thought that in spite of what Gabry had just said, the fact that he had indeed risked his life for his cousin might ease that burden on his conscience a little.

"At any rate, to me, this is infinitely more than that," said Thierry, and they walked on in silence, but content.

And so they came to the bank of the Moselle. The ferryboat was on the other side.

"How do we get it?" Claudine asked, gazing across the water.

Gabriel smiled. He dropped her hand and cupped both his own to his mouth, sending a ringing call across the river.

"Hol' iwer!"

An answering shout and she saw the ferry-boat beginning to move towards them.

While it was on its way Gabriel took Claudine's hand and led her a little way off from the others.

"Concordia," he said, and Claudine found how much she liked hearing again this nickname he had given her at Villerange, "I expect you are in as much of a daze as I am at this sudden meeting, but before we go much further away from Luxembourg, I want you to understand that you can still go home. I could find trustworthy people in Meyring, I am sure, who would take you up the river and escort you to your aunt in Trier, or all the way to Hautefontaine. It was brave of you to come here with Thierry, in case I got away, but I know it is asking a great deal to expect you to leave your home and everyone you love, just for me."

Claudine looked up at him with her serious straight gaze, her grey eyes like iridescent moth's wings.

"Is that what you want me to do – go home?" she asked.

"It's not what I want," he answered, "but it's what I think might be best for you. What I want is for you to come with me, for us to get married as soon as we can, even though we shall have no proper home and that soon I shall have to go and join the Archduke. Of course I should find somewhere for you to stay as near us as is safe, and you would have Lisel; Norbert and I would come back as often as we could, be sure of that. And before Thierry leaves I would try to get him as witness to a new will, so that if anything happened to me, you would not be left stranded in a foreign land. But I realise that what I want is selfish enough to make me suggest that, till the war is over, you would be better off with your father and mother at Hautefontaine."

The possibility of a return home took away from Claudine all wish for it. And the fact that Gabriel had been thinking about their future in such concrete terms as wills and where she would live when he was back in the Austrian army, suddenly gave it a reality that was reassuring. It was not the actual provision he had planned which reassured her, so much as that he had planned it, and she felt that must be a special effort for someone as careless of the future and of his own safety as Gabriel d'Erlen.

"You don't have to decide at once, my love," he said, watching her silent face. "But perhaps before we leave Meyring."

"I have decided," said Claudine calmly. "I am coming with you."

She had spoken so simply that he seemed hardly to realise what she had said.

"You will? You are sure, Claudine?"

Claudine smiled. "Yes, I am going to fly with you after all," she said.

Round his shoulder she could see the boat drawing in to the landing stage.

"How can you think I could go back and live at home, not knowing what was happening to you?" she went on. "The war might go on longer than you expect, and anyway, I love you *now*."

"Oh, blessed angel! And why can't I kiss you *now*?" he said in delight, putting his arm round her. They were standing facing one another.

Claudine laughed. "No, Gabry – because too many people are watching," she said. "But let me give you back your ring – it meant so much that you sent it to me, last night."

She put up her hand to unbutton the neck of her coat, and pull out the chain on which she had strung the ring again, this morning.

But Gabry put his hand over her hand. "Is it where it was before?" he said softly. "Keep it there, then, for me, till I can give you another which will fit your finger better."

His back was towards the group on the quay and shielded her from them. He took her hand for a moment, fondling it, and then kissed it. Claudine was so close that she could lean her head against his shoulder and she felt his face against her hair.

Then Thierry called out, "Come along, you two turtle doves! Our ark has arrived."

They went back, hand in hand, to take their places on the ferry.

It was only the Moselle they crossed, but the Rhine was to come. It was a fine day, late in winter, with a feeling that the light was stronger, that spring was coming, even if there was as yet no sign of it on the ground.

But half way over Gabry put his hand in his pocket.

"Look what I've found in the woods, Concordia."

He put them in her hand – snowdrops.

Masquerade
Historical Romances

Intrigue excitement romance

Don't miss
November's
other enthralling Historical Romance Title

THE ABDUCTED HEIRESS
by Jasmine Cresswell

Burdened by an enormous inheritance and scheming
guardians, Georgiana Thayne has managed to avoid
an enforced marriage to her Cousin Freddie for six
long years by acting out a childish masquerade. Just
when she can hide no longer behind a pretence of
plainness and stupidity, the notorious Marquis of
Graydon — disreputable and mysterious —
unexpectedly intervenes by abducting Georgiana, and
thus preventing her detested marriage.

Infuriated by his cynical use of her to further his
own schemes, Georgiana resolves upon revenge.
Unfortunately, she begins to realise that if Freddie
had resembled her devilish kidnapper, she would not
have objected to being married in the first place . . .

You can obtain this title today from your local paperback
retailer

Masquerade
Historical Romances

Intrigue excitement romance

THE SHADOW QUEEN
by Margaret Hope

It was Kirsty's uncanny — and potentially dangerous — resemblance to Mary, Queen of Scots, that saved her from an arranged marriage with Dirk Farr, the gipsy laird. But had she only exchanged one peril for another?

ROSAMUND
by Julia Murray

Sir Hugh Eavleigh could not forget Rose, the enchanting waif who had tried to rob him on the King's Highway. Then he learned that she was really Lady Rosamund Daviot — his prospective bride!

Look out for these titles in your local paperback shop from 14th December 1979

Bring back the age of romance
this Christmas
Masquerade
Historical Romances

*Intrigue * excitement * romance*

Eight of your favourite titles in two
specially-produced gift packs.

THE RUNAWAYS *Julia Herbert*

ELEANOR AND THE MARQUIS *Jane Wilby*

A ROSE FOR DANGER *Marguerite Bell*

THE SECRET OF VAL VERDE *Judith Polley*

PURITAN WIFE *Elizabeth de Guise*

THE KING'S SHADOW *Judith Polley*

THE FORTUNE-HUNTER *Julia Herbert*

FRANCESCA *Valentina Luellen*

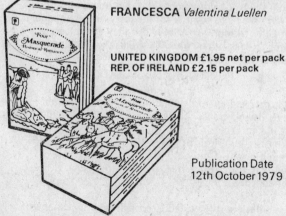

UNITED KINGDOM £1.95 net per pack
REP. OF IRELAND £2.15 per pack

Publication Date
12th October 1979

191

Masquerade
Historical Romances

Intrigue excitement romance

BLACK FOX
by Kate Buchan

A king's word can create an alliance — but not love, and
Isabel Douglass is determined to escape an arranged
marriage with the fierce, proud Master of Glencarnie
who regards her with open contempt as a mere political
pawn. Yet a Fate stronger than either seems to draw
them inexorably together . . .

RUNAWAY MAID
by Ann Edgeworth

Emphatically refusing Sir Joseph Varley, the suitor of
her parents' choice, Miss Robina Westerley takes her
destiny into her own hands — and runs away. Rescue
from the worst consequences of her impulsive action
always seems to come from the lofty, imperturbable
Sir Giles Gilmore — yet how can they ever mean anything to each other, when he thinks that Robina is
only a lady's maid?

FOUNTAINS OF PARADISE
by Lee Stafford

Shipwrecked en route to Bombay, Emily Hunter
finds herself transplanted from Victorian England to
an Indian Prince's harem. Her only hope of escape
from her luxurious prison is the handsome Prince
Dara himself — and yet, when the Mutiny breaks
out that will set her free, she feels reluctant to leave
her captor . . .

These titles are still available through your local paperback
retailer.